Michael Underwood and The Murder Room

>>> This title is part of The Murder Room, our series dedicated to making available out-of-print or hard-to-find titles by classic crime writers.

Crime fiction has always held up a mirror to society. The Victorians were fascinated by sensational murder and the emerging science of detection; now we are obsessed with the forensic detail of violent death. And no other genre has so captivated and enthralled readers.

Vast troves of classic crime writing have for a long time been unavailable to all but the most dedicated frequenters of second-hand bookshops. The advent of digital publishing means that we are now able to bring you the backlists of a huge range of titles by classic and contemporary crime writers, some of which have been out of print for decades.

From the genteel amateur private eyes of the Golden Age and the femmes fatales of pulp fiction, to the morally ambiguous hard-boiled detectives of mid twentieth-century America and their descendants who walk our twenty-first century streets, The Murder Room has it all. **>>>**

The Murder Room
Where Criminal Minds Meet

themurderroom.com

Michael Underwood (1916–1992)

Michael Underwood (the pseudonym of John Michael Evelyn) was born in Worthing, Sussex and educated at Christ Church College, Oxford. He was called to the Bar in 1939 and served in the British army during World War Two. He returned to work in the Department of Public Prosecutions until his retirement in 1976, and wrote almost 50 crime novels informed by his career in the law. His five series characters include Sergeant Nick Atwell and lawyer Rosa Epton, of whom is was said by the *Washington Post* that she 'outdoes Perry Mason'.

Reward for a Defector

Michael Underwood

An Orion book

Copyright © Isobel Mackenzie 1973

The right of Michael Underwood to be identified as the author of this
work has been asserted in accordance with the Copyright, Designs and
Patents Act 1988.

This edition published by
The Orion Publishing Group Ltd
Orion House
5 Upper St Martin's Lane
London WC2H 9EA

An Hachette UK company
A CIP catalogue record for this book is available from the British Library

ISBN 978 1 4719 0794 4

www.orionbooks.co.uk

CHAPTER 1

'WALTER can't understand why the government doesn't do something about it!'

Charles Ashmore blinked and assumed a cautious expression. He hadn't the faintest idea what it was the government were failing to do to Walter Quigley's satisfaction. But then his senior partner was one of those people to whom the shortcomings of others were a manifold source of criticism.

Charles glanced down the table to where Walter Quigley, distinguished in appearance and, at this hour of the evening, relatively mellow, was holding forth on the need for firmer action against what he called the nation's disruptive cliques. The recipient of his views, the wife of Charles Ashmore's doctor, wore an attentive, albeit slightly glazed, expression.

He forced his attention back to Celia Quigley who was sitting in the place of guest of honour on his right. He thought her a quite astonishingly silly woman whose conversation seemed largely to consist of repeating her husband's prejudices. How Walter, who was anything but stupid, could ever have come to take her as his third wife would remain a mystery! Particularly after seeing his first two marriages end in the Divorce Court. But certain men of Walter Quigley's age—he would be sixty-five next birthday —were prone to behave ridiculously when it came to women. Presumably, because their glands refused to grow old with the rest of their bodily tissue. But, so far as Charles was concerned, there had been an alarming malfunction of his senior partner's glands to have induced him to marry Celia, who was thirty years his junior and resembled a carp.

'Walter says the firm has never worked harder for less profit than nowadays,' she said, dashing a spot of lemon soufflé from her chin.

1

'The overheads have certainly increased enormously,' Charles agreed, 'but I don't think I have any personal cause for complaint.' And nor does Walter, he felt like adding, seeing that he now comes in only three days a week and continues to take a lion's share of the profits. Not that he begrudged him this. After all Quigley, Smith and Co. had been founded by Walter's grandfather and Walter was the third generation senior partner. It was just that he, Charles, always found it embarrassing to affect near poverty when he had a comfortable house in Knightsbridge and a cottage in Sussex, with staff at both establishments.

'Of course, you're a wealthy widower with your children off your hands,' Celia Quigley said with a note of faint resentment. 'It's different for us.'

Charles made a vague *'c'est la guerre'* gesture. He was aware of Walter's alimony commitments, though he also knew him to be still extremely comfortably off.

His gaze went round the table again. This was definitely not being one of his more successful dinner parties and the fault lay with the Quigleys. Walter discoursed rather than conversed and he doubted whether Celia had ever made an original remark in her life. Having them really was rather tough on other guests.

'Walter tells me you're not enjoying spending your days at the Old Bailey.'

'No, I'm not. I feel like a fish out of water in that place. Thank heaven, it's only once in a decade that any of our clients fall foul of the criminal law. And the present case is, of course, particularly worrying.'

'I think it's rather exciting the firm having a spy for a client!'

Charles frowned. 'You really oughtn't to say things like that, Celia. I mean about Evelyn Ragnold being a spy. The trial is still on and if he's acquitted then you're guilty of a gross slander.'

Celia Quigley looked amused. 'You're just like Walter, you're both so discreet.'

Charles' faint surprise at her husband's apparent sense of discretion was removed as she went on, 'I usually have to prise the juicy bits of scandal out of him! Anyway, I don't

2

imagine there's any doubt that Major Ragnold did pass information to the Russians, is there? Whatever the jury say!'

Charles shrugged, at the same time willing the man on Celia Quigley's other side to relieve him of her conversation. And in some miraculous way it actually happened.

The last subject he wanted to discuss at dinner was the Ragnold case and the last person with whom he would ever wish to discuss it, anyway, was Celia Quigley.

As he had said, the case was worrying and he also found it extremely distasteful. Had Sir Wilfred Ragnold, who had been his client for years, not pleaded with him so fervently to look after his son's defence, he would have declined on the perfectly reasonable ground that it was too far removed from their normal run of work and that his interests would be better looked after by a firm versed in criminal work. It was one thing to defend their clients on motoring charges, though even this was not a very frequent occurrence, but it was quite another to undertake the defence in a State trial of such grave proportions. For there was no doubt that if Evelyn Ragnold was convicted, he would probably be sent to prison for the maximum fourteen years.

Briefly, the allegation against him was that, while working in the Ministry of Defence, he had passed to the Russians details of NATO contingency plans. He had done this, it was said by the prosecution, as a result of contacts made when he served as assistant military attaché in Moscow two years previously. It was hinted by the prosecution that he'd become compromised while there and was subsequently acting under blackmail.

The trial had been going three days and was likely to last another week, but Charles felt as if the case had been overshadowing his life for much longer. As indeed it had, for Ragnold had been arrested three months ago. The hearing before the magistrate had been a month later and now the trial had just begun at the Old Bailey. Both sides had wanted the matter disposed of as quickly as possible and, because also of its national importance, this had led to the machinery whirring into action, as it still could when the will was there and the public interest was sufficient.

Charles had briefed an eminent silk and a scarcely less

eminent junior at the outset and had instructed both to appear at the Magistrates' Court, though the proceedings there had been little more than a formality.

Defending the son of an old friend and client on such a charge—one could hardly think of one more opprobrious for an army officer to face—was distasteful enough, but when you added to that the atmosphere of hostile suspicion which enveloped the whole case, the burden became well nigh intolerable.

It was one thing to be aware that your country supported a security service, it was another to find yourself personally embroiled to the extent that your professional and private life was fully, if discreetly, probed and picked over, your movements surreptitiously watched and your telephone tapped. Charles had no evidence of the last matter, but a sixth sense told him that it was so.

And all because he, a most respectable solicitor in a most respectable firm, was defending someone who was accused of being a traitor to his country. Of course, he'd always known it happened in a general sense, but it was very different when it was happening to you personally. Very different indeed!

He had wondered once or twice whether he was being made the subject of extra special attention on Sarah's account. Sarah, his daughter, had spent a couple of years in the Foreign Office not long after she left school. It had been one of those hush-hush branches into which the so-called right types of girl are recruited as secretaries.

By birth and education, Sarah might have qualified, but her personality soon revealed her to be a misfit. And worse, an irreverent misfit. She had been declared unsuited for the work and had departed with relief on all sides. Since then she had worked in a small publisher's office to her own fulfilment and to the apparent satisfaction of her employer. For a time she had lived with her father, but now she shared a flat with two other girls, and was liable to drop in on him without warning once or twice a week.

Could it be, he had had occasion to wonder recently, Sarah had raised such question marks by her conduct in the Foreign Office that her family had become suspect? But suspect of what? It all seemed ludicrous and quite inconceivable, though Charles knew enough to be aware that nothing was regarded as being inconceivable in the twilight world of spying and counter-spying. Nevertheless, he still doubted whether the polite but distant manner in which he was treated by those who had prepared the case against Evelyn Ragnold flowed from anything to do with Sarah.

But it was all very different from the cosy, if contentious, realm of civil law in which he was most at home.

The meal came to an end and they adjourned to the upstairs drawing-room where coffee and liqueurs were waiting. Having done his duty by having Celia Quigley next to him at dinner, Charles had no compunction in sitting himself next to someone else for the final stage of the evening.

He had barely sat down, however, when the telephone began to ring. A minute or two later, Burden, the husband of the married couple who looked after him, appeared at the door.

'A gentleman wishes to speak to you, sir. He didn't give his name.'

Charles made a face, excused himself and went out of the room.

'I told him you had guests, sir, but he said it was very urgent.'

'I'll take the call in my bedroom,' Charles said and ran upstairs. But when he lifted the receiver, it was only to hear the dialling tone.

Puzzled he returned to the drawing-room to find Burden still hovering on the landing.

'Whoever it was had already rung off,' he said.

'I meant to tell you, sir, he was speaking from a call-box.'

Charles frowned. He wondered who on earth could be phoning him from a public call-box at half past ten at night. It was most unusual. All his friends had telephones of their own. It could only mean a wrong number (admittedly, that was common enough), a crank or someone in trouble.

'It was definitely a man, was it?' he asked, Sarah coming to mind as the most likely person to call him in trouble.

'Yes, sir. A foreign gentleman by the sound of his voice.'

5

To Burden, who had once been a fully-fledged butler in a ducal home, all males were either gentlemen or just men according to an esoteric yardstick which Charles had never attempted to understand.

'Most probably it was a wrong number,' he said. 'He didn't actually ask for me by name, did he?'

'Yes, sir.'

'Then it wouldn't have been a wrong number! Anyway, if it's really urgent, he'll call back. The fact that he hasn't done so already seems to indicate the contrary.' Despite his words, however, he was puzzled. 'If the phone rings again, I'll answer it myself.'

'Very good, sir.'

He rejoined his guests, but was relieved when forty-five minutes later the first couple rose to go. Another couple also got up and he saw them out. He hoped that Walter Quigley and his wife wouldn't stay much longer. They always were the last to leave, Walter apparently feeling it his duty to pass final judgement on the evening in the absence of his fellow guests.

'Excellent dinner,' he said as Charles re-entered the room. 'Interesting company, too. It's such a rarity to find good conversation these days. That Mrs. Fieldhouse was avid to hear my views on judicial reform. Gather she sits as a J.P. on some country bench.' He cast a doting glance at his wife. 'Well, poppet, it's time we were off, too. Leave Charles to get his beauty sleep for another day at the Old Bailey.'

'He only goes because he wants to, he'd send one of the clerks otherwise,' Celia Quigley said with a sly smile.

'That's where you're wrong, poppet. In fact that's the difference between a firm such as ours and a lot of these firms that do nothing but criminal cases and have clerks flying around the Courts scarcely knowing a damn thing about any of their cases. It's always been a rule in Quigley, Smith that counsel has the benefit of being instructed by a qualified person, more often than not by a partner.'

Charles nodded. 'It was your father who taught me that when I first joined the firm, Walter.'

They reached the front door.

'By the way,' Walter said smoothly, 'I shan't be in the office tomorrow, Charles. Celia wants me to take her down to Brighton for the day.'

'Have a nice time.'

He was in the act of closing the door behind the departing guests when the telephone began to ring. The nearest instrument was on the hall table, but something compelled him to dash up to his bedroom to take the call.

His hand was trembling slightly as he lifted the receiver.

'Hello.' His tone was wary.

Immediately he heard the succession of hectic pips indicating that his caller was in a public kiosk. They stopped abruptly, there was a click and a voice said urgently:

'Charles. This is Kurt. Kurt Menke. I need your help quickly, Charles. They're chasing me now. If they find me, they will kill me.'

CHAPTER II

FOR a second or two, though it seemed much longer than that, all Charles could think of was: 'What on earth is Kurt Menke doing in London?' But this was clearly not the moment for social pleasantries.

'Where are you?' he asked.

'At Piccadilly Circus. In a telephone box. Please. Charles, will you come?'

'Yes, I'll come at once. Go to the Piccadilly Hotel and wait in the foyer. I'll meet you there.'

'Piccadilly Hotel. Where . . . ?'

'It's only a few yards from where you are. It's a big hotel. You'll be all right there.'

'All right, I go now.'

The line went dead and Charles replaced his receiver. For a minute, he just stood staring at it. He had sounded very authoritative on the telephone, but now doubts started to assail him. Should he have told Kurt to stay where he was and have phoned the police? Would he now arrive at the hotel in time to see Kurt's body being carried out to an ambulance?

He came out of his momentary trance and picked up his overcoat. The sooner he reached the Piccadilly Hotel, the sooner he would know the answers to the succession of questions which were flashing through his mind like lights on a pin-table.

It was a frosty February night, but his five-year-old Rolls started immediately. He'd be there in under ten minutes. Most of the traffic at this hour was moving out of the centre and he'd have a clear run.

His last contact with Kurt Menke had been the usual Christmas card, which was almost their sole contact these days. Occasionally, they exchanged a letter, though this had become rarer as the years passed. And yet he was the person to whom Kurt naturally turned when in trouble. It was curious, however, that his German friend had given him no advance notice of his visit to England! Well, the explanation of that, as of much else, would soon be forthcoming.

He did a mental calculation. Yes, it must be nearly fifteen years since he had seen Kurt. It was certainly well before the erection of the Berlin Wall as there had been no problem for Kurt to visit Charles at his hotel in West Berlin. At that time, Kurt was struggling to keep his small business going against State pressure. Charles couldn't even remember now exactly what the business was. He'd gained the impression that he'd had a number of different jobs since the end of the war, all of them lowly and none of them very satisfying. This had saddened him as Kurt was intelligent, as well as having considerable charm, and Charles had remembered the year he spent living with the Menkes learning German when Kurt, who was his own age, had been his constant companion. They had discussed their futures on countless occasions. Although only eighteen at the time, Charles already knew that he wanted to be a lawyer, but it was the glamour of an international lawyer which then appealed to him. He saw himself flitting from capital to capital conducting multilingual negotiations. How different his practice had been in fact! And Kurt had wanted to enter the diplomatic service, though Hitler who had just come to power was already casting shadows over that ambition.

As he drove past Hyde Park Corner, Charles reflected that it was the true friendships of one's youth which remained the firmest even when they were not sustained by frequent contact. The older you grow, the fewer the friends with whom you share the past. He and Kurt shared a very important slice of each other's pasts and the annual exchange of a Christmas card was enough to keep their friendship cemented.

With a quickening heart beat he drew up outside the hotel. The commissionaire stepped forward with a questioning expression.

'I'm just picking up a friend. I shan't be half a minute.'

'That'll be all right, sir.'

Charles bounded across the pavement. Even as he pushed his way through the small throng just inside the door, he spotted Kurt standing in an alcove beyond the reception desk, glancing nervously about him.

Charles gave him a wave and Kurt sprang from his alcove as though propelled by a charge of dynamite.

As they shook hands, Charles said, 'I've got the car just outside.'

Kurt nodded, but didn't say anything. Charles noticed that he looked anxiously about him as they crossed the pavement. He huddled himself in the front passenger seat while Charles went round to get in the other side. Not until the car had drawn away from the kerb did either of them speak and then it was Kurt who broke the silence. Turning towards Charles, he said in a tense voice:

'You are wondering what has happened? It is quite simple. I have run away.'

'Run away?' Charles echoed, while his mind sought to digest the implications of what Kurt had said.

'I am running away from my country. I do not wish to go back to the D.D.R. Not any more ever.'

Charles thought for a moment as he negotiated a right turn at the bottom of the Haymarket—and decided to assemble his questions with lawyer's logic. There were so many to ask, but he'd better start at the beginning.

'When did you arrive in London, Kurt?'

'Six days ago. I come with the delegation of hygiene officers. You have read perhaps?'

'I'm afraid not.'

'Your Ministry arrange for us to visit here and to see your fine sewers and things.'

Charles gave a laugh. 'You're serious? Anyway, what do you know about sewers, Kurt?'

'Please don't laugh, Charles. I am very serious. I am a member of the Secretariat of the Union to which our delegates belong.' He paused and gave Charles an appealing look. 'Oh, I am sorry, Charles. I should not have spoken to you like that. You who are my rescuer. It is just that I am all tight nerves. I agree, it is funny to think of Germans coming to visit your sewers. But many of your sewers are an example to other cities. In Brighton, they are very good! It is true that I do not myself know anything of the technicalities. I am just a union official. A bureaucrat.'

'Where have you been staying?'

'At a hotel near Queensway. We stay all altogether and are watched. We must share bedrooms and not go out alone.' He glanced out of the car window and released a long sigh. 'But now I am free. I have been planning this escape for so long, Charles. As soon as I knew there was a chance of my coming with the delegation, I have secretly hoped and planned. But if I had appeared too keen, they might have suspected and I would not have been allowed to come.'

'I take it it was you who phoned earlier in the evening?'

Kurt nodded. 'From a telephone box not far from the hotel. While I was there, I saw some of our delegation go past. One of them was our watchdog. I panicked and ran out and took the underground train to Piccadilly Circus.'

'You said on the phone that you'd be killed if they caught you. Who is the person you actually fear?'

Kurt was silent for a time. 'How can I explain?' he said at length in a suddenly depressed and weary tone. Hitching himself round in the seat and looking straight at Charles, he went on, 'Perhaps I have an accident. Who is to tell? Accidents can be arranged. Perhaps I am taken back to East Germany as a sick man. Then I shall be tried in secret and sent to prison and no one will know what has happened to Kurt Menke. No one will like to ask. All these things are possible, Charles. But you do not think so?' His voice held a note of veiled hysteria.

'No, I'm sure everything could happen as you say. I don't doubt you for a moment.'

There were enough defections from the countries of eastern Europe for everyone to be aware of the fuss which immediately broke out. The angry demands for the defector to be handed over, followed by the denunciations and rumbling threats when he wasn't. Clearly sewer experts were regarded no differently from writers or ballet dancers when it came to defecting.

A sudden thought occurred to Charles and he automatically lifted his foot off the accelerator.

'Do any of your people know about me?'

Kurt shook his head. 'No. That was why I could not tell you I was coming, and why I could not get in touch with you until I was ready.'

'That's all right then. Otherwise there might be someone on the doorstep, I suppose, when we get home.'

'There would be,' Kurt said grimly.

A few minutes later, Charles drew up outside the house. Kurt looked along the pavement in both directions before getting out and hurried inside as soon as Charles opened the front door. Under Kurt's watchful gaze he double-locked and bolted it behind him.

'Is that you, daddy?' a voice called out from upstairs. Kurt went immediately as tense as a cat about to spring.

'It's all right. It's my daughter, Sarah.'

'Where on earth have you been at this hour of night? I thought you were having a dinner party here. I thought you must have . . .' Sarah suddenly appeared at the top of the stairs. 'Oh, I'm terribly sorry, I didn't know you had someone with you.'

'Kurt, meet my daughter, Sarah. Sarah, this is Kurt

11

Menke whom you've never met but whom you know very well by name.'

'Yes, of course.' Sarah came running down the stairs with a welcoming smile. 'My brother and I grew up on stories of the Menke family and all that depravity in Berlin you and daddy used to sample as students.'

'Take no notice of her, Kurt.'

But Kurt Menke was smiling for the first time since Charles had picked him up.

'Daddy hadn't told me you were going to be in London,' Sarah said over her shoulder as she led the way up to the drawing-room.

'I got in touch with him first this evening,' Kurt said.

As they entered the room, he walked across and gave the heavy curtains a sharp pull to ensure there were no cracks through which unseen eyes could peer. Then he sat down with his back to the window and smiled again.

'Kurt was here on an official delegation and has defected,' Charles explained to Sarah.

'Oh, now I understand,' she said slowly, looking at their visitor with fresh interest. 'What are you going to do?'

The question was directed at her father who was pouring drinks at a glass-topped table set against the wall.

'We haven't yet discussed that, though I imagine the choice of action is strictly limited. Obviously, we must notify the authorities. It's just a question of which ones.' He handed Kurt a large Scotch and Sarah a Kümmel. 'I suppose it had better be the police and they'll know which of the security branches to contact.'

Kurt who didn't appear to have been listening to this exchange suddenly looked up and said, 'Perhaps I may stop with you for a few days, Charles, until I find work and somewhere to live?'

'That won't rest with you or me, I'm afraid. It depends what the security people say. I imagine they'll want to ask you a few questions.'

It didn't seem the moment to inform Kurt that he was likely to spend the coming days, if not weeks, in some form of protective custody while he was pumped for information and his bona fides were being established.

'But we won't do anything till the morning. Do you agree that's best, Sarah?'

She nodded. 'Even if "the Service" never sleeps, there's no reason why other people shouldn't,' she said with a grin, her tone giving 'the Service' a mock salute. 'Would you like me to see if the spare room's made up? I expect the Burdens have gone to bed by now.'

'Thanks, darling. It's usually all prepared for the unheralded guest, but perhaps you would make sure everything's there.' He accompanied her to the door. 'Incidentally, you've not said why you looked in to-night?'

'No particular reason. Just thought I'd catch you between dinner folk and going to bed. How's the case going?'

'All right, I suppose.'

'But not much fun?'

'Certainly not that.'

'You're getting your fill of publicity.'

'I am?'

'Don't sound so horror-struck! No, not you personally. I meant the trial generally.' She paused and then gave her father a fond, affectionate look. 'You really are getting caught up in cloaks and daggers.' Before he could reply, she said, 'He's quite different from what I expected. It's difficult to believe you're the same age. I mean, of course you're good-looking, but he's a real dish. That mop of honey-coloured hair, and not a line on his face . . . I'd better go and see to his room.' She turned and shot upstairs.

'Your daughter is like you, Charles, she is very simpatica,' Kurt said, as Charles came back into the drawing-room. 'And now I would like to go to bed. Tomorrow . . .' He paused. 'Tomorrow I start a new life. I will yield myself to your authorities.'

'Yes,' Charles said slowly. 'I'll make the necessary arrangements in the morning before I go out. I'm afraid I can't stay with you long after breakfast as I have a case which requires my attendance at Court and I'll be there all day. But don't worry, I'll make sure everything's in train before I leave.'

'Your daughter will be here perhaps?'

'No. She works for a publisher. Anyway she doesn't live here. She has a flat of her own.'

They moved towards the door and Kurt took a sudden deep breath.

'Free air, Charles! You cannot know how wonderful it is to breathe free air!'

Charles smiled abstractedly. He was thinking how miraculously the ordinary human mind adjusted to new circumstances. At least, one half of him felt as though it had been coping with defecting friends all its life. The other half, it must be admitted, felt bemused by sense of utter unreality.

Kurt's voice broke in on his thoughts. 'Your case at the Court, it is one of your causes célèbres?'

Charles glanced at him sharply, but his expression belied any guile. 'It's a trial at the Old Bailey,' he said in a dismissive tone. Then feeling that he was being unnecessarily stuffy, he added, 'I don't know whether you've read the English papers while you've been here?' Kurt nodded. 'Then you must have seen about the trial of an army officer on an Official Secrets Act charge.'

'Oh, la la, yes.' Kurt appeared embarassed. 'I must not ask you about that. I am sorry, Charles. You forgive me?'

'There's nothing to forgive.'

At that moment Sarah came down to announce that the spare bedroom was all ready.

'I'll be off now, daddy,' she said, kissing her father's cheek. 'Once things are sorted out I expect we'll meet again, Mr. Menke. I'll look forward to that.'

'And so shall I,' Kurt said, bringing his heels together and kissing her hand. 'But please call me Kurt. Though I like *Mr*. Menke, it makes me feel already English.'

Charles led the way to the bedroom. As he ushered Kurt in, he noticed that he turned the key to find out if the lock was working.

'I lock the door tonight,' Kurt said in a tone as though he was expecting Charles to remove the key.

'I'll call you about half past seven,' Charles said.

'Good-night, Charles. And thank you. I apologise if I am a bad guest.'

14

'You're not exactly an ordinary guest!'

'I hope I do not bring trouble to you.'

'I see no reason why that should happen.'

'You English are always so polite,' Kurt said with an amused smile. 'But I wonder if your thoughts are the same as your words.'

They shook hands and Charles retired to his own bedroom. He fell asleep almost immediately, but woke up quite suddenly in the middle of the night, his mind assailed by premonitions. Though all was silent, he switched on the bedside light and looked at the time. It was half past four.

Getting out of bed, he went across to the door and opened it. He tiptoed across the landing and put his head against the door of Kurt's room. From inside came the sounds of deep breathing.

Reassured, but feeling faintly foolish, he regained his his own room and went back to bed.

CHAPTER III

HE had hardly knocked on Kurt's door the next morning before it was flung open to reveal a fully-dressed Kurt.

'I am ready for the day,' he said with a cheerful smile. 'The sooner things happen the more I am pleased.'

'Did you find everything you needed?'

For answer, Kurt held up both hands to frame his face. 'Do I not look clean?'

Charles grinned. 'Yes, you look very spick and span. I haven't shaved yet. Breakfast will be ready in twenty minutes' time.'

'And then?'

'I've decided to phone up someone I know in the Home Office. He's a senior official and he'll advise us on the next step.'

15

'Good! Good!'

A night's rest had obviously done marvels for Kurt's morale. He might be somebody embarking on a special treat rather than a defector about to plunge into the labyrinthine process of security checks.

Charles had only the haziest notion what lay in store for his guest, but he doubted whether it would be all light and joy.

'You phone him now?' Kurt enquired eagerly.

'I'm afraid he won't be in his office much before ten. You'll just have to be patient. Go downstairs and look at the paper and I'll join you in a few minutes.'

'No, I wait in the bedroom,' Kurt said with one of the abrupt changes of mood to which Charles was becoming used.

Kurt was silent at breakfast and ate with obvious impatience to have the meal finished, leaving bits of food on the side of each plate he used.

'If this person is not in his office until ten o'clock, will you have time to speak to him before you go?' There was an edge to his voice as he spoke.

'Yes.'

'But your trial?'

'I'll phone my office to say I'll be late arriving at Court.'

'You can do that?'

'Certainly.'

'And the judge won't be angry?'

'He won't even notice. I'm not an advocate in the case. I'm a solicitor, I brief the barristers and they do all the talking in Court.'

Kurt shook his head in bewilderment.

'I still do not understand, but I am glad you do not go before you speak to the person in the Home Office.'

Charles felt faintly nettled it should even have entered Kurt's mind that he would leave him high and dry. But then he told himself that you had to make allowances for the nervous tension someone in his position must be experiencing. It was only natural that he was obsessed with his own problem and should, in consequence, display a few of the egotistical shades of his character.

While Charles finished his own breakfast, Kurt prowled

16

restlessly about the room, occasionally making sorties to the window and peering cautiously out.

'I go and wait in my room,' he said suddenly and disappeared out of the door, somewhat to Charles' relief.

A few minutes later Burden came to clear the table and to enquire if the guest would be using the spare bedroom again tonight. Charles said it was most unlikely, but he'd phone home later in the day and let the Burdens know.

Just before ten o'clock he shut himself in his own bedroom and dialled the number of the Home Office. He asked to be put through to Mr. Edwards. His secretary answered. Yes, Mr. Edwards was in——Who wanted him——? Hold on a moment, please—.

'Hello, Edwards, this is Charles Ashmore.'

'Good morning, what can I do for you?' enquired a crisp, urbane voice.

'Who should somebody who has defected from an Iron Curtain country get in touch with here?'

'Is this an academic or a practical question?'

'Practical.'

'Would the country be East Germany?'

'As a matter of fact it would. But how on earth did you guess?'

'I just thought it might be. I'd heard someone had disappeared from a delegation of theirs visiting this country. They reported his disappearance to the police late last night. They thought he might have had an accident.'

'He hasn't. He's in my spare bedroom.'

'I suggest he stays there and I'll arrange for somebody to come round and see him. As you probably realized, there are various formalities to be gone through. I take it you'll be available, too. They'll obviously want to ask you a few questions as well.'

'I rather wanted to get to the Old Bailey as soon as possible, but I'll stay if it's necessary.'

'I think it'd be advisable,' Edwards said crisply. 'Of course, you're involved in the Ragnold case, aren't you?'

'Yes.' There was a short silence, before Charles went on, 'I'd like to explain how I come to be involved in this other matter.'

17

'Yes?'

'I've known him since I was a student in Berlin and spent a year with his family. That's the only reason he has turned to me.'

'Sounds very natural.'

There was something disconcertingly detached and un-ruffled about Edwards' tone. They were members of the same club where Charles knew him as a luncheon com-panion. He had always regarded him as one of the manda-rins of Whitehall and this first official contact with him had done nothing to dissolve the impression.

'Well, I'd better get something moving on this. I'll call you back as soon as I can and let you know what the form is.'

'Thanks. I seem to have phoned the right person, any-way,' Charles said drily.

'You could have done worse.'

After ringing off, Charles went across to Kurt's room to give him a progress report. Kurt listened to him in silence and then glanced impatiently at his watch.

'Incidentally, do you have any money?' Charles asked suddenly.

'One pound and about thirty of your pence.'

'I'd better give you some. You'll be needing to buy various things. A spare set of clothes for a start.'

'If you give me fifty pounds, I will repay you when I start working.'

'I haven't got fifty, but here's twenty to be going on with. Anyway, I can get more to you in due course.'

The telephone rang and Charles hurried back to his room.

'Mr. Ashmore?'

He recognized Edwards' secretary's voice. 'Yes.'

'I have Mr. Edwards for you.'

'Ashmore? That's all fixed. A couple of chaps will be call-ing on you very shortly. I'd better tell you their names. One's Wragg, the other's Bowyer. Probably see you at lunch one of these days.'

'Hold on a moment,' Charles said as he realized Edwards was about to ring off. 'I haven't told you my address.'

'8 Edgeworth Terrace, S.W.3, isn't it?'

'Yes, that's it.' Charles was unable to keep the note of surprise out of his voice.

'Good. Well, they'll be with you shortly.'

The line went dead leaving Charles with the feeling that Edwards could add omniscience to his other qualities. A quiet, unspectacular sort of omniscience at that.

* * * * *

They were in the drawing-room when the car pulled up outside. Each of them had been consciously listening for it as the slow minutes ticked by.

Charles rose and went across to the window. A man was getting out of the driving-seat of an Austin 1300 which had pulled up immediately behind the Rolls. The man glanced at the numbers on the doors and then up at the window where Charles was standing. His expression was wholly impassive. Meanwhile, another man had emerged from the front passenger seat. Where the first man was chunky—he looked a bit like an army officer not yet used to civvies—the other was lithe, in need of a haircut, and was wearing a pair of country suedes which contrasted with the fashionably narrow trousers of his dark suit.

'It is they?' Kurt asked stiffly.

'I think so, yes, I'll go down and let them in myself.' It had suddenly occurred to Charles that he should check their credentials before admitting them. It seemed unlikely that his own lot could yet have got on to Kurt's tail, but it was not the moment to take any chances.

'Mr. Ashmore?' the shorter man asked as Charles opened the door. 'My name's Wragg and this is Mr. Bowyer.' He was holding an envelope in his hand and now thrust it at Charles. 'You'd better be satisfied that we're who we say we are.'

Charles took the envelope which was marked 'Secret' and had 'Home Office' printed on it. Inside was a short letter signed 'Jocelyn Edwards' saying that Wragg and Bowyer were calling pursuant to the recent telephone conversation between himself and Charles.

'I take it our friend is still here?' Wragg said.

'Yes, he's up in the drawing-room. I'll take you to him.'

19

Kurt was pacing up and down when they entered the room. He turned and stared at the visitors, who stared back at him. Charles felt impelled to speak.

'Kurt, these are the two gentlemen from the Home Office. Mr. Wragg and Mr. Bowyer.'

Kurt brought his heels together and gave them a small bow. Then in a strangely formal voice, he said:

'I, Kurt Menke, wish to renounce my citizenship of the Deutsche Demokratische Republik and to seek asylum in the United Kingdom.'

It was clear that he had prepared this small speech in advance. Bowyer wore a faintly amused expression, but Wragg's face was as neutral as a piece of grey granite.

'I don't suppose you have your passport with you by any chance?' Bowyer said in a languid tone.

Kurt shook his head. 'All our passports were kept together.'

Bowyer nodded. 'Yes, they usually are. I just wondered.'

'I gathered from Mr. Edwards that Kurt's disappearance from his hotel had already been reported to the police?' Charles said.

'Correct,' Wragg said without taking his unwavering gaze from Kurt's face.

'Of course the D.D.R. has no accredited diplomatic representation in this country,' Bowyer observed, with a slightly deprecating smile.

'When he phoned me last night, Kurt felt that his life could be in danger. I imagine the threat still exists?'

'I imagine so,' Wragg said in a detached way. 'However, we shall be able to give our friend all the protection he needs.'

Kurt inclined his head in acknowledgement. 'It is not clear to me,' he said. 'You gentlemen are security police?'

'Not exactly,' Wragg replied, while Bowyer's amused smile came on again. 'That is to say, we're not police officers, but we are members of the security service.'

'But different branches,' Bowyer added with a look which seemed to say 'and make what you like of that if it amuses you.'

The two men exchanged a look and then Wragg said, 'If our friend is ready, we could go.'

Charles, who had expected they'd both be interrogated there and then, was taken aback.

'It's better at our place,' Wragg added, as if reading his mind.

'You don't want me to accompany you?' Charles enquired.

'No need. Though we'll probably get in touch with you in the next day or so.'

'I suppose I mustn't ask where you're taking Kurt?'

'Don't worry, he'll be well looked after,' Wragg said rather like a headmaster reassuring the parent of a new boy.

Indeed, as Charles now looked at Kurt he felt the analogy was not inapposite. Kurt had an expression which was a mixture of apprehension and excitement. He came across to Charles with hand outstretched.

'Thank you, Charles. I shall always remember your kindness and we shall see each other soon. These formalities will not take long, huh? And then you will be my first guest in England.'

He shook Charles' hand warmly while Wragg watched impassively and Bowyer's small amused smile re-formed.

When he let them out, he stood at the front door and watched the car drive away. This time Bowyer was at the wheel and Kurt and Wragg were in the back.

He wondered to what anonymous hideout Kurt was being taken and in what circumstances he would see him again.

He hoped his own part in the affair was finished, apart from answering a few questions. Something told him, however, that this was facile optimism.

CHAPTER IV

CHARLES ASHMORE arrived at the Old Bailey about twenty minutes before the luncheon adjournment. An officer of the Special Branch at Scotland Yard was giving evidence of

21

various searches of Ragnold's home and office desk. He had found nothing which was damaging so far as Charles' client was concerned and his evidence was largely uncontroversial.

The Court, which had been in closed session when hearing evidence of the actual secrets Ragnold was alleged to have passed, was now packed. It seemed to Charles that the only spectator interest lay in staring at the man in the dock as though by doing so with sufficient concentrated effort one would be able to glimpse a hammer and sickle engraved on his heart.

Charles was aware that various people glanced at him with curiosity as he crept into his place at the large table in front of Counsel in the well of the Court. The Director of Public Prosecutions' representative and, next to him, one of the security service's legal men both peered in his direction, as did the Detective Chief Superintendent of the Special Branch who was the officer in charge of the case and who was sitting on the opposite side of the table.

He presumed that the word must have got round. This was hardly surprising as the Court was stiff with members of the security services. It seemed that each individual cell had an interest in the Ragnold trial and had sent along its representative. It hadn't occurred to him until he reached Court, however, that his involvement with Kurt Menke was likely to make him an object of further suspicion with those concerned in the prosecution of Ragnold. Perhaps it was naïve of him, he reflected, not to have expected it.

At one o'clock, the Court rose and Charles turned to speak to Martin Ainsworth Q.C. and Dennis Traver who were his Counsel in the case.

'I'm sorry about this morning,' he said to Ainsworth, 'but I hope you got my message.'

'You've missed nothing and though your presence is always fortifying, it happens we required little fortification this morning,' Ainsworth said with a smile. He glanced around him at the rapidly emptying Court and said in a lowered voice, 'I had the distinct impression from our various faceless friends in attendance that something new had been brewing. One can always tell, their nonchalance becomes even more studied as they flit to and fro.'

'It could be that I'm the cause of that,' Charles said and went on to explain shortly what had happened.

'Yes, I can see that could cause them a bit of a flurry,' Ainsworth said.

'I hope you don't think it'll embarrass Ragnold's defence.'

Ainsworth shook his head. 'We'll face that if it looks like happening. At the moment, I can't see how it could—other than by a wild stretch of the imagination.'

Ainsworth and Trevor drifted away and Charles braced himself for a visit to Ragnold in the cells below the Court. He usually went either at the beginning or the end of the luncheon adjournment, though it required a considerable effort of will to do so. It was all right if there was some specific aspect of his defence to discuss, but he found a social visit most trying. The prosecution's allegation against Ragnold lay between them like a solid wall and was about as inhibiting as that to any sort of contact.

Secretly, Charles had little doubt that Evelyn Ragnold had done what was alleged. Whatever verdict the jury might return, prosecutions of this nature were not brought unless those concerned were a hundred per cent certain of their case. Charles shared their certainty and he suspected that Ainsworth and Traver also shared it, though this had never been so much as hinted at in all their conferences and discussions.

And for Charles there was something wholly repugnant in accepting that a man of Ragnold's birth and education—an officer and a gentleman even in this trendy, egalitarian age—had passed his country's secrets to a potential enemy.

Charles, who, on the whole, had a fairly liberal viewpoint, had tried to tell himself that he'd have been as shocked if the so-called secret information had been passed to, say, Spain rather than Russia, but he wasn't completely successful.

He found Ragnold sitting on a wooden chair in his cell munching smoked salmon sandwiches. As an unconvicted prisoner he was allowed to have food sent in at his own expense if he wished, and Charles had arranged for two rounds of smoked salmon sandwiches to be sent across each day from the pub opposite.

Ragnold rose as he entered the cell. 'Hello. I got your message saying you'd be late this morning.'

'Yes, I'm sorry about that, but I gather from Mr. Ainsworth there were no dramatic developments.'

'No, thank God!' Ragnold said with a short laugh. 'I had a letter from my father this morning and he asked me to pass you his regards.'

'He's not coming to London in the near future?'

'No, I've asked him to stay away until it's all over. Same thing with Marion. She and the children are staying near father at the moment. It's much better they should keep out of the way. No need to involve them in the nasty business.'

He spoke with the same composure he had shown from the outset. When he spoke about his trial, it was with the objectivity of an observer. Charles had assumed this could be his conscience at work. If you can't get away from your misdeeds, at least you can try and keep them at arm's length.

As Charles watched him, Ragnold picked a crumb of brown bread from the jacket of his dark blue suit and dropped it on the floor. He had a trim figure and always looked neatly attired. Not a hair of his head or of his small military moustache ever appeared out of place.

'Feel I ought to offer you a sandwich . . .'

'No, don't worry. I'll get something to eat in a few minutes.'

'They're particularly good today. Must be a fresh bit of salmon, they've got in.' He picked up the last sandwich and began eating it. When he had finished, he neatly folded the piece of grease-proof paper in which they'd been wrapped and picked up the midday paper which lay on the table. 'I still try and pick out a few winners,' he said with a smile, 'even though I can't back my fancy.'

Charles gazed at him in covert amazement. Guilty or innocent, how could he behave with such an apparent lack of concern about his fate? It wasn't natural. His nerve must be of steel, which in itself pointed towards his guilt. If he was innocent, the strain must have driven him mad by now. The fact that he had failed to break down, under lengthy and skilfully conducted sessions of interrogation was a further pointer.

From the start, Charles had had the impression that the

authorities knew much more than they were either able, or willing, to prove. Evelyn Ragnold himself must be aware of this better than anyone. He must know all about the sub-terranean channels through which secrets filter, and the dangers of exposure through a defector from the country whose interests you were serving. It was a hair-raising game in which lives could be quietly forfeited when some hidden manipulator decided that State interests required it.

'Well,' Charles said uncomfortably, 'I thought I'd just come and see that everything was all right. Anything you want at all?'

'Could you bring me some more cigarettes do you think?'

'Yes, I'll do that. Nothing else?'

'No, that's all, thanks.'

When Charles returned to Court in the afternoon, he was handed an envelope by the security service legal adviser.

'I was asked to give you this,' he said in a tone which clearly repudiated in advance any responsibility for the contents.

Charles opened it and extracted the folded note inside. It bore a box number at the top and said simply:

'Would like to call on you this evening at eight o'clock. Hope that's convenient. J. Wragg.'

CHAPTER V

BEFORE making his call on Charles Ashmore, Wragg went to see the head of his section, a man named Brigstock.

Brigstock was dedicated to his job, was totally unaware of creature comforts and his room was about as cheerful as a station waiting-room on a winter's night. It contained the range of utility government furniture which managed to look like discarded junk after one week's use. Not that any-thing less than £1m face-lift could make their building less institutional. It had been a block of luxury flats once upon a time, but now it had the seedy, down-at-heel appearance of all buildings converted into government offices. Unlike others, however, it provided no indication as to its use and of the hundreds who passed by its entrance each day, there was probably not one who knew what went on inside. Though some may have wondered why its ground-floor appearance was of a building fortified against a bottle-throwing mob.

Brigstock was composing a tricky memo to the Director-General when Wragg entered and was glad of the interruption.

'How's Menke?' he asked.

'I've been with him all day and he's still sticking to his story.'

'You haven't indicated anything to him . . .?'

Wragg shook his head. 'No, we've just gone backwards and forwards over the same ground. I've given him no reason to suppose that we suspect anything.'

'When are you proposing to take him down to the country?'

'Tonight.'

'So you'll be down at "Lakeside" all tomorrow?'

'And the day after and the one after that. But I'll come up to town some time each day.'

Brigstock stuck a hand inside his shirt and scratched his chest.

'There's not much we can do, I suppose, save go through the usual motions.'

Wragg nodded. 'That's right.'

'What about Ashmore? Is he in the clear?'

Wragg was silent for a while before answering. 'It does seem a remarkable coincidence that Menke should come over right in the middle of the Ragnold case.'

'With Ashmore the common factor?'

'Exactly.'

'What do we know about Ashmore?'

'We'd never heard of him until he came on the scene in the Ragnold case. We made the usual discreet enquiries to ensure he was a safe person to have a sight of the various documents in the case and nothing was turned up against him at all. He appears to be a respectable, upper-crust solicitor who normally never goes near a criminal court.'

'Any political affiliations?'

'Votes Tory, but seems to belong to the liberal end of party thinking.'

'Ah! I suppose he wasn't by any chance a Communist at the university?'

'As I say, we have nothing recorded against him.'

'We must find out just what he knows about Menke.'

'I intend doing that this evening.'

'Once we're satisfied he's in the clear, we might be able to put him to use.'

'I've thought of that.'

'It really is a puzzler,' Brigstock said, having a further scratch at his chest. 'Let's hope Bowyer's man in Berlin can get something back pretty soon. Because it seems to me that until he does, all we can do is play a waiting game.'

'Agreed. Though it's possible that we may discover a chink in Menke's armour ourselves if we push hard enough.'

'What sort of man is he?'

'He's all right. Speaks pretty good English—says he learnt it at school and university before the war and has always kept it up. Reads English books and newspapers . . .'

'How does he get hold of English newspapers in the D.D.R.?' Brigstock asked sharply. 'They're not on general sale.'

Wragg gave a slight smile.

'Before I could ask him that, he told me how, until recently, he had been limited to reading *The Morning Star*, but now you were able to buy an occasional copy of *The Times* in East Berlin.'

'True?'

'True.'

'Does he seem nervous?'

'No more than his situation would indicate.'

'Has he said what he has in mind for the future?'

'He would like to settle in one of what he calls our cultural cities in the west country.'

'And do what?'

'He would like to write articles for newspapers, but

realizes he would need a bread and butter job as well. He mentioned personnel management.'

'So all in all he gives the impression of a minor official in the general sewage workers' union who has sought freedom and peace under Her Majesty?'

'Correct.'

'What about the rest of the delegation? What's been their reaction to their defecting comrade?'

'They've clammed up. No one is saying anything. But they've decided to continue their tour.'

'You mean it's been decided for them?'

'Yes.'

'No chance of nobbling one of them?'

'I would say none at all. They're clearly bewildered and alarmed by what has happened.'

'I wonder how much any of them knew about Menke?'

'There's no way of finding out.'

'No way?'

'No way that won't create more difficulties than we want at the moment.'

'I'm not sure that I'm not prepared for difficulties as the cost of finding out a little something about our friend Menke. I'd like to think about it.'

There was a silence while Brigstock slowly drained the dregs of a cup of coffee which had been on his desk for over an hour. Wragg watched him.

'You'll take Menke down to Sussex after you've seen Ashmore?'

'That's my intention.'

'Who's with him at the moment?'

'Wilson and Hall are both at the flat.'

'Last time I went to the flat, I got a very odd look from one of the other tenants on our floor. I wonder if it isn't time for us to move?'

'That block has advantages. Lift, two staircases and three outside fire escapes. All the tenants are middle-aged and well-off and they're not much interested in us, as long as we don't disturb them at night. Which we don't. They think we're something to do with government hospitality.'

'It describes our use of the flat very well.' Wragg made a

move towards the door and Brigstock went on, 'Ring me from the flat before you go down to Sussex.'

'Here or at home?'

'Here. I'll probably sleep here tonight.'

* * * * *

At about the same time as Wragg and Brigstock were talking, Bowyer was conferring with his section head in another building.

'I've sent a message to V that we must have more information about Menke's defection as a matter of urgency.'

The head of section smothered a yawn and nodded, though without apparent interest. Bowyer's manner always tended to irritate him and he invariably reacted by displaying indifference to what he was telling him.

'V?' he queries languidly, though well aware who was being referred to.

'Vogelgesang, our contact in East Berlin.'

'Oh, yes, I'm with you. Bloody silly name for anyone to go under!'

Bowyer bridled. 'I think it's a rather cunning cover name. He was one of the lesser meistersingers in the Wagner opera. And our V has certainly sung well for us. You know what Vogelgesang means in German?'

'Yes, a warbling of birds.' Bowyer looked crestfallen. 'Well, let's hope he sings again,' head of section went on, 'and quickly. I'd like all this dealt with before the newspapers get hold of anything. Once it becomes a front-page story the whole thing becomes immeasurably more difficult. It's where the other side have such an advantage. Nothing gets printed unless they want it.'

'It's the difference between the free world and the dictatorships.'

Head of section nodded sourly. He didn't want any lectures on the essence of democracy from Bowyer. He wished he didn't find him such an irritating young man. He felt it was a sign of weakness in himself to become rubbed up the wrong way so easily. Unfortunately, it was only a week or two since he'd enquired of 'personnel' when

Bowyer was due for another overseas posting and been reminded that he'd been back only nine months from his last.

'Who's looking after this end of the Menke affair at our neighbours?'

'Wragg.'

'Never heard of him.'

'He's good. A bit abrupt and he doesn't have any sense of humour, but he's a hard-working pro.'

'He sounds just right for Brigstock's section. Went to a meeting last week and Brigstock was there and he never stopped scratching. We all got showered in dandruff.'

'Wragg is taking Menke down to their Sussex hideout tonight.'

'That's up to them!'

'It's much safer for him there than in London.'

Head of section gave a testy sigh.

'I suppose V is not a double or anything kinky like that?'

Bowyer looked shocked. 'If you can be certain of anything it is that V is one hundred per cent clean.'

'And V kindly tells us in advance that Menke is going to defect,' head of section mused, 'and it all comes to pass.'

'V tells us much more than that,' Bowyer interjected.

'I know, I know. He tells us that Menke works for a section of the K.G.B. in East Germany.'

'The same section as V works in as a clerk,' Bowyer added eagerly.

'But what V can't apparently tell us is what lies behind this defection. Is it genuine—or is it a plant?'

'Not yet he hasn't been able to. But he's aware of the urgent need to find out and let us know.'

Head of section ran his finger tips along the underside of his desk as he gazed pensively across the room to the carefully curtained window.

'Once upon a time,' he said in a sad tone, 'I used to be stimulated by all the deviousness and the intrigue: by the moves and the counter-moves. But now I just wish everything would stay quite still for a time.'

'I'm afraid it's rather like wishing for the sea to stay still,' Bowyer said in a surprisingly sympathetic tone. 'But the sea is never still, not even when it looks flat calm. And it's the same in our job.'

Head of section looked up and nodded. At that moment, he felt quite warm towards Bowyer.

'Well,' he said slowly, 'if I were given any choice, I would choose to have Menke an unimportant sewerage official who has been won over by our drains.'

'It might be your choice, but I doubt whether it's the truth. In fact, I'm damned sure it's not.'

'So am I—unfortunately.'

CHAPTER VI

CHARLES ASHMORE got back to his office from the Old Bailey just before five o'clock, took one look at the pile of work awaiting him and decided that, as he wouldn't be able to get through it all, he wasn't even going to make a start. He would take it down to the cottage at the weekend. Apart from dining with friends nearby on Saturday evening, he was free of commitments and would soon make an inroad on it.

His secretary, Miss Acres, who had been with him for nearly twenty years, accepted his decision with her customary equanimity. She rarely bullied him, but when she did he knew it was time to yield.

When he reached home, he took a long hot bath, put on casual clothes and poured himself a stiff gin and french, which he drank while glancing through the evening paper.

The Ragnold trial, in one of its duller phases, had been relegated to an inside page. There was no mention of the Menke affair, presumably because neither side was yet ready for any publicity and the press had not nosed anything out for itself.

At half past seven he went downstairs to the dining-room and in solitary state dined off two poached eggs on toast, followed by gruyère cheese and an apple. All washed down by a pint of beer.

It wasn't the hour at which he normally chose to eat, but with Wragg coming at eight and with no indication as to how long he might stay, he had decided he had better eat early and light.

He had just finished his meal when the telephone rang. In the certainty that it was Wragg calling to say he'd be late or wouldn't be coming at all, he lifted the receiver with a chilly response already forming in his mind. But it was Sarah.

'Hello, daddy, how's the day gone?'

'It's still going, alas. I'm expecting a man named Wragg here in a few minutes' time.'

'Who's he?'

'Somebody from one of the branches of the security service. I don't know which.'

'What's happened to Kurt?'

'Wragg and another chap took him off this morning and I haven't heard anything since. Possibly I shall be told this evening.'

'It's quite possible they'll enlist your help over Kurt.'

'*My* help!' Charles sounded startled. 'I don't know what help I can give them.'

'Sometimes friends can elicit details which strangers—particularly professional interrogators—can't.'

'What sort of details are you talking about, my sweet?'

'You don't think they're going to accept Kurt's story at its face value, do you?'

'I've not thought about it very much. No, I realize they must check it, but I can't see that'll give them much trouble.'

Sarah was silent for a moment. Then she said, 'Don't forget you have a tame consultant on these matters in the family. I may be able to keep you straight.'

'I hope I shan't deviate.'

Sarah giggled. 'Anyway you know what I mean. And give me a ring later this evening and let me know about Wragg's visit.'

'You'll be in?'

'Yes, I'm washing my hair.'

Charles was smiling when he replaced the receiver. Sarah always managed to improve his mood whatever it had been before. And the present arrangement whereby they lived separately seemed, in a perverse way, to have further strengthened the bond of affection between them. With her penchant for collecting lame ducks, living under the same roof had provided its trying moments. Now, it was much easier to admire her philanthropy.

Apart from her salary from the publisher she worked for, she had inherited some money from her mother and so had what her father regarded as a reasonable but not corrupting income.

From a purely selfish point of view, he hoped she wouldn't get married and disappear out of his regular life. His son, David, who was two years older than Sarah and was a research bio-chemist, now lived with his wife and three children in California and had only been home once in the last five years. He, Charles, was due to go and visit them later this year and was eagerly looking forward to the trip. Though he had largely recovered from the death of his wife, to whom he had been devoted, Sarah was the only close family member left with whom he had regular ties and they meant a great deal to him.

Wragg arrived on the dot of eight o'clock and was shown up to the drawing-room by Burden.

'Drink?' Charles said when his visitor was seated.

Wragg glanced at the table on which the tray of drinks stood.

'Have you any beer?'

'Sure.' Charles went across to fetch the beer and to pour himself a weak Scotch. 'You haven't brought your colleague with you this evening?' he said, for want of conversation. There was something inhibiting about Wragg's manner that drove one into uttering platitudes.

'No.'

Charles handed him his drink and sat down opposite him. All right, Wragg was the supplicant, so let Wragg make the running.

'How long have you known Menke?' Wragg asked, with-

33

out acknowledging the glass of beer on the small table beside his chair.

'I first met him in 1934 when I went to Berlin as a student and stayed in the Menkes' home . . .'

'Whereabouts in Berlin did they live?' Wragg interrupted.

'Friedrichshain,' Charles said, hoping Wragg would have to ask him where that lay.

'What is now East Berlin,' Wragg said.

'Yes. But in those days it was almost central Berlin. It's where Kurt still lives. Not the same house, but the same district.'

'Yes. And you have kept in touch ever since?'

'Apart from the war years, yes. Though our contact has been somewhat tenuous of late. Not much more than an exchange of Christmas cards.'

'How many times have you seen him since the end of the war?'

'Only once when I was visiting Berlin.'

'When was that?'

'I don't recall the exact year, but it was before the wall went up.'

'And since then you have kept in touch by letter?'

'Yes. We've written to each other from time to time.'

'Which of you would initiate an exchange of letters?'

'I'm afraid it was usually Kurt.'

'Do you have any of his letters?'

'Good heavens, no. I don't keep letters once I've answered them and there was nothing special about his.'

'What sort of things did he write about?'

Charles frowned. There was something inexorable about Wragg's questions and as a lawyer he didn't much care for being on the receiving end of a cross-examination.

'I really can't recall,' he said a trifle testily.

'Did he tell you about his work, for example?'

'No. What's more, he never wrote anything that came anywhere near to expressing a political opinion.'

'But you knew what his job was?'

'After his own small business folded, I gathered he was—— Well, I'm not sure what I gathered, but I got the impression from somewhere that he was a clerk with the East Berlin municipality.'

'In what department?'

'I've no idea. Presumably, the department that looks after drains and sewerage.'

Wragg's expression remained gravely impassive. 'Did he refer to his family in these letters?'

Charles sighed. 'He didn't have much family to refer to. As you're probably aware, both his parents died during the war, his father in a concentration camp. His elder brother was killed fighting on the Russian front; his sister, Ruth, became a nun and is in Africa, and his other sister married a Peruvian and has lived in South America for the past twenty years.'

'Did you ever meet Menke's wife?'

'No. I gather it was a wartime marriage which broke up soon afterwards and that she and her child went to live in West Germany. Kurt never mentioned her in his letters after the break-up.'

'So he was pretty well alone in the world?'

'Apparently.'

'Did he ever mention a mistress?'

'No.'

'Might he have had one without your knowing?'

'He could have kept a harem without my knowing.'

'So what *did* he mention in his letters?' Wragg persisted.

'Plays and operas he'd been to. Holidays he was planning....'

'What holidays? Where to?'

'I remember his saying in one letter that he'd been to one of Bulgaria's Black Sea resorts.'

'Did he strike you as a contented person?'

'Yes. As I've said, he never voiced any controversial views in his letters and though we did keep in touch, I know next to nothing about his life since the war ended.'

'Were you surprised when he phoned you last night?'

'Very.'

'Did he ever strike you as someone who might one day defect?'

'What an extraordinary question!'

Wragg opened his eyes slightly wider. 'It seems a perfectly straightforward one to me.'

'Perhaps we live in different worlds.'

'Meaning?'

'Isn't it obvious?' Charles was becoming increasingly nettled, not so much by the questions as by the manner of his interrogator.

'I'd have thought,' Wragg said solemnly, 'that we're both interested in having the same sort of England to live in.'

'Probably.' He tried to sound indifferent to Wragg's concept of a desirable society.

'So what is your answer?'

'No, it had never occurred to me that he might one day defect, just as I imagine it never occurred to you and yours that Burgess and Maclean might defect.'

'They weren't friends of mine. Menke *is* a friend of yours.'

Charles felt he had been rather smartly scored off and grudgingly acknowledged the point by a sour little smile. His mood wasn't improved by the realization that Wragg was managing to bring out the worst in him.

'How is Kurt?' he asked.

'He's all right.'

'What will happen next?'

'It's too early to say.'

'There's no doubt that he will be granted asylum, is there?'

'That's a matter for the Home Office.'

'But I imagine they listen to what you tell them?'

'I hope so.'

'Why do you doubt Kurt's bona fides?'

'I'm paid to doubt, Mr. Ashmore.'

'But have you any *particular* reason for doubting Kurt?'

'Naturally, we have to be satisfied that he's no more than he says he is.' In a faintly portentous tone he added, 'The national interest requires that we should do so.'

'I just hope for Kurt's sake that any doubts you have about him will soon be resolved,' Charles said coolly.

Wragg reached for his glass of beer which he had left untouched, 'Cheers!' he said, to Charles' surprise. 'Do you go down to your cottage most weekends?' he went on to Charles' further surprise.

'As a matter of fact I do, but how did you know I have a cottage?'

'I suppose somebody must have told me,' Wragg answered vaguely. 'Will you be down there this coming weekend?' he asked, focusing his attention back on Charles with sudden directness.

'Yes.'

'I might ask you to help us.'

'In what way?'

'Have Menke over either Saturday or Sunday. All right?'

'Preferably Sunday.'

'Good. We'll bring him and fetch him again in the evening.'

'What's the object of this exercise?'

'To make him feel at home, shall we say. People in his position usually run the gamut of emotion in a very short space of time. A day spent in your company would, I'm sure, help him feel more settled.'

'A therapeutic visit?'

'Exactly. Take him for a walk in the English countryside. There's nothing more soothing than that.'

'To the mind, if not the feet!'

'Correct.'

Charles was puzzled. He was sure Wragg was keeping something back. That he had some additional reason for making his request. But it was not until his visitor got up to go that anything further was vouchsafed.

'How is the Ragnold trial going?' Wragg enquired, apparently out of the blue, as they reached the top of the stairs on their way down.

'It'll probably last most of next week,' Charles said, choosing to take the question literally.

'Did Menke ask you about it?'

'No, he certainly didn't! I believe I mentioned it to him when I was explaining that I might, if necessary, have to leave him here this morning.'

'Did he appear interested?'

'No. I think he said he'd read of the case in an English paper, but that was all.'

'If he asks you about Ragnold on Sunday, you will let me know, won't you?'

'Why do you think he will?'

'I don't know whether he will or not, Mr. Ashmore, I'd just like to know if he does. Come to that, I shall be interested to learn what he does talk about.'

'In effect, you're asking me to spy on a friend,' Charles said stiffly.

'Nothing of the sort. There are certain processes which have to be gone through and the sooner they're accomplished the better for everyone, not least Menke.'

'I still don't care for it. Supposing you misinterpret something I pass on to you that Kurt said—.'

'We shan't.'

'Well, I reserve the right to decide for myself what I tell you and what I don't tell you.'

'I shall rely on your sense of responsibility,' Wragg replied bleakly.

'Incidentally,' Charles went on, 'does it matter if he meets other people?'

'What other people?' Wragg's tone became suspicious.

'Neighbours—and the like.'

'On no account must they learn who he is. You can just say he's a German friend on a visit to England, if it becomes necessary to say anything.'

'And my daughter may drop in. She sometimes does at weekends. I take it you have no objection to her and Kurt meeting. They have done already.'

'That's your daughter who used to be in the Foreign Office?'

'It seems there's very little you don't know about *me*,' Charles observed tartly, 'even if Kurt's life is less of an open book to you.'

'You're being sarcastic,' Wragg said without rancour. 'I only know about your daughter because Bowyer recalled her.'

'Oh, I see.' He would ask Sarah about the slightly egregious Bowyer.

'I'll drive Menke over about twelve o'clock on Sunday. All right?'

'Where'll he be staying?'

'In the country, too. It's better to get them beyond the thirty mile limit from London.'

'Why's that?'

'None of the Iron Curtain diplomats and hangers-on are allowed to travel beyond thirty miles from the centre of London without permission from the F.C.O. It's a tit for a tat. Our people are subject to the same restrictions in their capitals. They're invariably given permission, but it means one has a check on who is where. Moreover one can turn nasty if someone is found outside without permission.'

'So you believe Kurt might be harassed by his own people?'

Wragg smiled thinly. 'In my job, Mr. Ashmore, one always prepares against every eventuality.'

As Charles watched him cross the pavement to his car, he wondered about him. If he had a home life, it must be a considerably neglected one if he worked as late as this every night and apparently at weekends as well. In Charles' view, it was unhealthy to be too dedicated, whatever the cause. It destroyed a sense of perspective, which was an essential element to stable living.

In Wragg's view, if Charles could have known, it was precisely that sort of sense of perspective which enabled all those who wished to subvert our way of life to flourish. Wragg saw himself a militant leader in the never-ending fight to preserve the country's liberties. Lower your guard for one second and the enemy moved in. For Wragg there were no greys: only blacks and whites. Or rather reds and non-reds.

Charles went back in and telephoned Sarah.

'My visitor has just departed,' he said in a sardonic tone. 'He really pummelled me with questions about Kurt. I think he regards us as a couple of communist conspirators.'

'I hope you took him seriously.'

'Of course I did.'

'I know his type. If you're facetious or flippant with them, you lay up trouble for yourself.'

'I was neither. Anyway, I think he was finally persuaded that I'm a true white man as he's bringing Kurt over to the cottage to spend Sunday. Thinks it'll help to sustain his morale.'

'I wonder—.'

'Wonder what?'

'Whether that's the real reason.'

'Oh, lord, you mean this could be some devious ploy?'

'Could be, but not necessarily. Anyway, would you like me to drop in on Sunday?'

'I think that'd be a fine idea. I'm sure Kurt would enjoy seeing you again.'

'I can't make it till the afternoon, as I'm going to a drinks party before lunch.'

'That's all right, come after that, provided you can still drive safely.'

Sarah laughed. 'It's a non-alcoholic drinks party. The host is a Buddhist. He doesn't drink or smoke, but he's still enormous fun.'

'What's he do?' Charles hadn't really meant to ask what he knew Sarah regarded as the irrelevant question of all time, but it slipped out and he awaited a rebuke.

'He's a copy-writer in an advertising agency.' There was a silence. 'You thought I was going to say he walked up and down Oxford Street in a saffron robe, chanting, didn't you?'

'What of it if you had?' he replied robustly, aware that Sarah was silently laughing at him. 'Incidentally, speaking of your friends, do you remember someone called Bowyer from your Foreign Office days?'

'Jerome Bowyer?' Sarah's voice held a note of surprised expectation.

'I don't know his first name, but he was the man who came here with Wragg this morning. And Wragg happened to mention this evening that Bowyer recalled having met you when you were in that outfit.'

'Yes, that's Jerome Bowyer. I knew him rather well at one time. We used to go out together ... He's *another* colourful character. I'm a bit surprised to hear he's still there.'

'Why?'

'Oh, he was even more irreverent than I was, and always

cheerfully unrepentant when he was hauled over the coals.'
Sarah giggled. ' "Come on, it's time to give one of the
sacred cows a slap on it's sacred bottom" was his favourite
war-cry.'

'I don't seem to remember your ever mentioning him.'

'I probably didn't,' Sarah said slowly. 'I could never
make up my mind about Jerome.'

'In what way?'

'How much I liked him. He was an extraordinary mixture
of charm, childishness and cold calculation.'

'How did he get into the Foreign Office?'

'He could speak four languages fluently. He got a first at
Hull University in theology of all crazy subjects and he was
absolutely fearless.'

'Was he intending to become a bishop when he read
theology?'

'No, I think he chose it because no one else did. That was
typical of him. He could probably have got a first in anything.'

'Well, if I meet him again, it'll be with more than normal
interest.'

'I'd be quite interested in seeing him again myself...
You might have had him as a son-in-law... Save that I
suspect he only proposed because he knew I'd say "no".'

'What would his part be in Kurt's affairs?'

'That's just what I've been wondering!'

CHAPTER VII

JEROME BOWYER stood in the middle of his tiny kitchen and
reached out for everything he needed to make himself a
plateful of spaghetti bolognese. He enjoyed cooking when
he wanted to think and tonight he wanted to think very
hard.

He was worried about V in East Berlin. He had a special interest in V, having recruited him himself, which meant that his own position was inexorably bound up in the agent's.

To say that he had 'recruited' him was to compress the long process of clandestine persuasion which had preceded V's enlistment as an agent for the British Secret Intelligence Service. Persuasion which had comprised both promises and duress.

V's recruitment had rightly been regarded as a coup and his flow of information had justified the build-up which Bowyer had given to his superiors.

Unfortunately, the channel of communication with V was laborious and it took time for messages to pass. This was inevitable in the circumstances, given that radio contact was impossible and that the various links in the chain were human beings unaided by technical devices for the crucial passage from East to West Berlin.

Now V was being put under pressure to dig out further information about Menke's defection and time was of the essence. It was vital that they should know the truth—and soon.

What was exercising Bowyer's mind as he thoughtfully stirred the simmering pan of spagetti was whether he shouldn't go to Berlin himself and make contact with V.

If he mentioned this to his head of section, he might or might not get approval. But even if he did, he would probably be given instructions which would run counter to his own concept of the task. In which case he would do it his own way and argue afterwards—or just tell them to stuff it. He felt he had quite a career as a freelance in his line of business and he suspected that it was also the acknowledgement of this by his superiors which sometimes made them swallow and overlook his wayward conduct.

If he was going to contact V, it would really be simpler to do it on his own without reference to anyone in the department. He could fly to Berlin one day and return the next. He'd use false papers to get himself into East Berlin and he'd contact V using the emergency procedure they'd worked out a year ago.

He smiled as he thought of the official stink this would cause when it became known. He might well be thrown out this time, though this would probably depend on the result of his visit. Results were regarded as the acid test in such a situation.

But there was another reason which made him contemplate an unofficial visit to East Berlin.

He had no reason to doubt V's integrity, but it would be useful to check. Agents are out in the cold on their own and anything can happen. Supposing he'd been rumbled by his own people and, instead of being quietly liquidated, had been put to use to send 'planted' information. It had happened before and it would happen again, Bowyer reflected grimly as he strained the pan of spaghetti.

And if he discovered that V *had* become a double, there'd be no pleas in mitigation to listen to, he'd kill him.

He felt a small tingle of excitement. All other considerations apart, he'd welcome a bit of action again. It was much more stimulating to do a job than to mastermind it for execution by others.

Also, he knew he was much better working on his own. He wasn't a good team man. He tended to infuriate his superiors and nonplus his equals.

He poured the bolognese sauce liberally over the spaghetti and carried his plate through to his bed-cum-living-room. Putting it down on the table he returned to the kitchen for a wine glass and the half-bottle of Valpolicella which he'd put out for his meal.

He wrinkled his nose in distaste as he ate—not at the food, but at his surroundings. It was a bloody awful little flat. Pokey and expensive. The only thing to be said in its favour was its central position and its general anonymity. Nobody was nosey about your visitors whether they were birds or secret contacts. And Bowyer was liable to have both sorts at any hour of the day or night.

It was a coincidence, Menke's link with Ashmore. He'd liked Sarah. She was something after his own heart, if not as unorthodox. He'd enjoy seeing her again. As he sipped his wine, he wondered whether he should make the effort to do so.

43

With his mind undecided, he finished his meal and took his plate and glass out to the kitchen and washed them up. If there was one thing he hated, it was the squalor of unwashed dishes in his vicinity. And 'vicinity' was the whole bloody little flat.

He returned to the living-room with a mug of coffee, put his feet up on the table and picked up the copy of Aquinas' *Summa Theologica* which was never far away.

When the telephone rang he cursed, despite being able to reach it without shifting his position.

'Bowyer?'

'Yes, Wragg.'

'Anything you can tell me?'

'Yes: I've just had an excellent supper.'

'You know what I mean.'

'Yes, I do and no, I have nothing to tell you.'

'I'm satisfied that Ashmore is in the clear.'

Bowyer refrained from saying that he'd been satisfied from the outset.

'Good. Where's our friend?'

'Safe and sound in the country.'

'Not fretting?'

'Why should he fret?'

'No pretendy fretting? If he's a plant, he'll do all that he thinks is expected of him.'

'If he's a plant, what the hell's he been planted for?' Wragg said in an unusually exasperated voice. 'I'm wondering whether your chap in Berlin hasn't . . .'

'I'd prefer you not to speculate in that way,' Bowyer interrupted coldly. Then in his more normal jaunty tone, he went on, 'Watch and pray, that must be our motto for the time being. You watch and I'll pray.'

He grinned as he pictured Wragg's expression at the other end of the line. But it was Wragg's own fault, he shouldn't have stepped out of line by voicing doubts about V. It was none of his business. Just as Menke's interrogation was none of his, Bowyer's, business.

Though he reckoned that, given a free hand, *he'd* extract the truth from Menke soon enough.

CHAPTER VIII

CHARLES was standing at the sitting-room window looking out when the car drew up in the lane outside. A log fire was blazing behind him and the delicious smells of a Sunday lunch had percolated through from the kitchen where Mrs. Tidmarsh was busy cooking.

Despite these cosy reminders of his secure and comfortable circumstances, he felt a slight chill as he watched Wragg and Kurt get out of the car and approach the cottage.

He put down his glass and went to the front door to greet them.

'I'll leave our friend with you,' Wragg said as though delivering a child at a party. And, indeed, Kurt wore the air of a slightly sulky child.

'Come in and have a drink, won't you?'

Wragg shook his head. 'No thank you. What time shall I come and pick him up? About half past six all right?'

'Yes. I shall be going back to town tonight, so six-thirty will be fine. 'Wragg nodded and had turned on his heel when Charles had a sudden thought. 'Can you give me a phone number where I can get in touch with you if necessary?'

Wragg turned back. He pulled a piece of paper out of his pocket on which he scribbled a number and handed it to Charles.

'This is a London number,' Charles said with a frown.

'Correct. Just ask for me and you'll be put through.'

Seconds later the car started up and he drove off.

Charles found that Kurt had already gone inside and followed him. He was staring moodily at the leaping flames of the fire.

'I can tell you need a drink, what'll it be?'

Kurt looked up with a rueful smile. 'I hope I am not rude, Charles, but that Wragg is not simpatico. He is stupid and I become most cross.'

'Well you're shot of his company for a few hours, so relax and enjoy a quiet English Sunday. Sherry? Gin? Scotch?'

'I would like very much some gin.'

'Anything with it?'

'Just a drop of water.'

Charles poured out a large gin and added a small amount of water. It looked pretty lethal to him, but if it was going to help Kurt unwind, so much the better. He gave himself another gin and tonic.

'Where have you driven from today?' he asked when they were both seated.

'I am being kept prisoner at this farm,' Kurt said in a fresh burst of indignation. 'I do not know quite where it is, but not many miles from here. Perhaps ten or twelve. It is bloody. It is worse than the dungeons of your Tower of London. It is cold and damp and that Wragg does not even notice. He would not notice if he were in an iron box in the lake and the water spilt in.'

'It's only a temporary measure, I'm sure,' Charles said soothingly. 'Also it's for your own safety.'

'It is for my own safety that I die of pneumonia?'

'You're safer in the country than you would be in London,' Charles replied. 'You told me yourself that your life was in danger.'

Kurt took a gulp of his drink, licked his lips and drained the glass, which he then jiggled in an ostentatious manner. Charles took the hint and fetched him another.

'Is there anyone else at this farm other than Wragg and yourself?'

'There is a cook and a man who does things. But all day it is just Wragg and his questions. I am sick of him.' He tossed back another swig of nearly neat gin. 'I think perhaps I make a mistake. In East Berlin, I am warm and do not have questions all day long.'

'But do you have freedom?'

'Freedom! Freedom! It is in the mind. I tell you, Charles, the only freedom I want is freedom from Wragg. If I am to be treated like this, I do not stay. I am sorry, I have made a big mistake, but I do not stay.'

'Have you told Wragg that?'

'No, but I shall tell him soon if I am not treated properly. I am not a criminal. I have risked everything to stay in England and I expect to receive some respect. But from that Wragg, no!'

Charles decided that another gin was called for. Kurt was certainly acting the prima donna and, though he didn't feel sorry for Wragg, he could see both points of view.

However you looked at it, the act of defection was traumatic and it was understandable that the mood of defectors in the early stages should swing wildly from intense exhilaration to black despair. The mental pressures must be enormous. Those, like Kurt, who clearly expected immediate red carpet treatment, were inevitably outraged at finding themselves in near protective custody and undergoing long sessions of interrogation.

'Tomorrow,' Kurt said as Charles handed him his refilled glass, 'I demand to see the employers of this Wragg. I shall say that you, my lawyer, have advised it.'

Charles looked up sharply to find that Kurt was grinning.

'I am sorry, Charles. I promise now to be a good guest. Your cottage is charming and your gin is excellent. I am already feeling much happier. What are we going to do?'

'After lunch, I thought we might go for a walk. It looks like being a nice afternoon and the countryside round here is beautiful.'

'Yes, a walk. I would like that very much. Where do we go?'

'We could take the car to the bottom of Chanctonbury Ring and walk up on to the Downs.'

Kurt nodded keenly. 'It will be safe?'

'It was Wragg himself who suggested our going for a walk,' Charles said. 'Whatever you may feel about him, I'm sure he wouldn't intentionally expose you to any danger. If he didn't think you were safe here, he wouldn't have allowed you to come.'

'He is stupid.' Kurt said flatly, his mouth turned down at the corners like a thwarted child's. Then his expression cleared. 'But I shall be all right with you, Charles. I know it.'

Mrs. Tidmarsh poked her head round the door to announce that lunch was on the table.

'I hope you're hungry, Kurt,' Charles said heartily as they sat down to roast lamb, roast potatoes, cauliflower with a cheese sauce and brussels sprouts.

--

47

'You have so much when you are alone?' Kurt enquired in a tone of comic wonderment.

'No, but Mrs. Tidmarsh enjoys cooking a proper Sunday lunch and I didn't know how they might be feeding you.'

'It is for pigs,' Kurt said equably.

During the meal, Charles kept the conversation on neutral subjects. He told Kurt about his son in California and about the history of the cottage whose first owner had reputedly been a discarded mistress of Charles II.

The lamb was followed by plum tart and the plum tart by cheese. Kurt's appetite, at any rate, was unimpaired by his experiences.

'Your daughter, Charles, how is she?' Kurt enquired when they were back in the sitting-room having coffee.

'You may see her. She said she might look in around tea-time.'

'Then we must not delay our walk,' he said, tossing back the brandy which Charles had given him and springing to his feet.

Fifteen minutes later they were driving down the Horsham to Worthing road. Kurt, who had fallen into silence, kept glancing behind him, so that Charles eventually felt drawn to comment.

'I don't think you need worry about the car behind. It's just a couple out for a Sunday afternoon jaunt.'

He had observed the car in his rear-view window when they were a few miles out of Horsham and it had remained about fifty yards behind the Rolls ever since. It was a new Volvo, being driven by a man. Beside him was a woman wearing a blue hat.

'Why does he not pass us?' Kurt asked edgily.

'From the look of his car, he could still be running it in. Anyway, this is British Sunday afternoon driving. Leisurely and sedate.'

'If you stopped, he could pass you.'

Charles gave a silent sigh. Kurt's mood seemed as variable as the weather itself. 'Certainly, if it'll make you happier.'

A quarter of a mile farther on, Charles pulled off the road and had hardly done so before the Volvo sailed past. The woman passenger gave them a casual look, but the man didn't turn his head.

'Now, are you satisfied?'

Kurt nodded. 'I am sorry, but suddenly I am afraid.'

'Tell me Kurt,' Charles said slowly, 'why should anyone want to kill you? If I may say so, you don't sound important enough to warrant such drastic treatment.'

At first, Charles thought Kurt was not going to answer and he wondered if he had offended him by his question. Then in his most serious voice, he said:

'I explain. But not now. Just trust me, Charles.'

A silence fell, not broken until Charles pointed a finger throught the windscreen. 'That's Chanctonbury. We're going to climb up there.'

A few minutes later, he parked the car and they both got out. Apart from an initial nervous glance about him, Kurt seemed fairly relaxed again. He even patted a large black dog that came frisking up with tail wagging.

The sky was grey with just a faint touch of yellow to the south to hint at the sun's whereabouts. But it was dry and the air was fresh and crisp.

About half-way up the track which led to the large clump of trees marking the highest point on the Sussex Downs, Kurt paused and looked back at the road below where they had left the car.

He inhaled a lungful of air and expelled it noisily.

'You were right, Charles. It is good here. So peaceful— and so beautiful in a typic English way. Not grand; nor baroque if you follow me, but so . . . what is the word?'

'Unostentatious?'

'Yes, without fuss.'

'You should have a glimpse of the sea when we reach the top,' Charles remarked, setting off again.

'It is good for you too, Charles, being in the free air after all week in the Court,' Kurt said enthusiastically. 'I read some more about this Ragnold process. What is this man doing telling things to the Russians?' His tone was indignant. 'He must be worse than a fool. He do it for money, yes?'

'I don't know why he did it—*if* he did it,' Charles said warily.

49

'I do not understand *if*. He has done it and now he is tried, is that not so?'

'The prosecution are seeking to prove that he did it, but the defence is a denial of the charge. The jury will decide when they've heard all the evidence whether the prosecution have proved the charge beyond a reasonable doubt.'

Kurt listened in silence to this brief exposé of the essence of an English criminal trial.

'He will be executed, I think not?' he said after a pause.

'He can't be. Capital punishment has been abolished in this country. In any event, the charge which has been preferred against him carries a maximum of fourteen years' imprisonment.'

'You know him well?' This after another pause.

'He's my client.'

'But you do not like him?'

'I didn't say that. Our relationship is purely professional.'

'But you have met him many times now, so you like him or you do not like him, hein?'

'You seem very interested in him,' Charles said aggressively. It was bad enough being subjected to Wragg's cross-examination, but to be on the receiving end of Kurt's questions was intolerable.

'Such people are always interesting,' Kurt said in an unabashed tone, 'but we talk about something else if you wish.' He stopped and sniffed the air like a pointer picking up a scent. 'Yes, this is good, Charles,' he remarked happily. 'I am feeling better all the time. I tell you something that I notice in London! No flag-poles!'

Charles looked puzzled. 'No flag-poles? There's one on top of almost every building.'

Kurt shook his head in amusement. 'In East Berlin, every balcony of every apartment has a flag-pole. Anyone who does not fly a flag when he is told will be noticed, then it is not good for him. So you see, I like no flag-poles. In England if I want to fly a flag I do, but no one make me. That is freedom.'

Charles smiled doubtfully, but decided not to disturb this naive view of freedom. Maybe we didn't yet have to fly flags when we didn't want to, but there were enough other infringements of personal freedom in one's daily life. What's more they increased each year, always for the so-called good of society as a whole. Presumably flag-flying in East Berlin was also ordained in the cause of the people's well-being. It was all a matter of degree.

They reached the large round clump of beech trees which crowned the summit of their climb.

'We'll go round this side,' Charles said, 'and get a look at the sea.'

About seventy yards further on he stopped and waited for Kurt who was lagging behind.

'That's worth the climb, isn't it?' he said pointing south towards the coastline. 'Even on a grey winter's day, it's a splendid view.'

Kurt nodded. 'Ist schön,' he said, slipping naturally into his own tongue.

They stood like two explorers gazing out over an undiscovered land, their backs to the great trees which formed Chanctonbury Ring. There was a wind and the scrape of branch against branch among the thickly clustered trees provided a natural accompaniment to the feeling of agreeable melancholy Charles always experienced when contemplating a sweeping landscape.

He was aware of a small rattle of loose stones behind him and heard Kurt give a grunt. But before he could even turn his head, an arm had shot under his left one and its hand had come up behind his head forcing it forward. At the same time, his attacker's right hand had seized the left lapel of his jacket and was pulling it tight across his windpipe. He struggled but as ineffectively as a lamb seized by a golden eagle. He was held in a vice and felt the blood pounding in his head as his vision became a red blur. Then he passed out.

When he came to, he had no idea where he was. He felt sore all over and he could only swallow with great discomfort. He also had difficulty in focusing his eyes and coloured spots danced in front of them.

He pulled himself up into a sitting position and slowly realised that he was still on Chanctonbury Ring, but had been pulled about ten yards inside the cover of the trees. He looked at his watch, but the face was blurred and the hands appeared to be in a different position each time he peered at it.

Rising shakily to his feet, he glanced about him, but there was no sign of Kurt. He walked to the edge of the trees and emerged into the stronger light. The spots before his eyes had thinned out and he was able to decipher the hands on his watch. It was a quarter to four.

He tried to work out how long he must have been unconscious. It couldn't have been more than six or seven minutes, though it could have been as many hours or weeks from his feeling of disorientation.

He looked around to see if anyone was near, but the only sign of human life was a group of people almost a mile away. Two adults were walking along a ridge while three children and two dogs romped around them. Just silent, distant puppets.

Slowly as his mind began to re-function, he realized he must try and find out what had happened to Kurt. It was unlikely that he had been kidnapped, if only because no one in their proper mind would plan a kidnapping at such a spot. And if he hadn't been kidnapped, he was probably not far away.

Stepping back inside the cover of the trees, Charles peered about him. He called out Kurt's name, but his voice seemed just to blow back in his face.

He moved deeper in and shouted again, but without response. After about five minutes, he began to realise the futility of his search. He'd better get to a telephone as soon as possible and raise help.

But it would be dark by the time anyone came and there'd be even less chance of finding Kurt—alive or dead.

It was while he was still standing indecisively in the middle of the trees that he thought he heard a human groan in one of the sudden silences which followed when the wind dropped for a few seconds.

Quickly he called out Kurt's name, but received no answer. Then he heard the groan again. It was more distinct this time and came from somewhere to his right. He moved in the direction and there suddenly was Kurt.

He was lying on his back in a shallow chalky excavation.

His eyes were closed and his face was covered with blood. Indeed, there was blood everywhere. It bespattered the loose chalk behind his head like a bright red syrup.

As Charles stared, appalled at the sight before him, Kurt stirred slightly and gave another groan. Charles knelt down beside him and gently lifted his head. The eyelids fluttered and suddenly Kurt was looking at him.

'Do you think you can sit up, if I give you a hand?'

Though Kurt said nothing, he appeared to understand and between them he was got into a sitting position. He put a hand up and gingerly touched his face.

'You look a bit of a mess,' Charles said. 'Wait here and I'll try and find some water. There's a new pond not far off once I get my bearings. Let me have your handkerchief.'

When he returned ten minutes later with both their handkerchiefs soaked in water, Kurt had moved and was sitting propped against a tree.

He still looked dazed, but allowed Charles to clear off the worst of the blood from his face. There was a gash on the back of his head which Charles cautiously bathed.

'Do you think you can manage to walk? It'll be downhill.'

Kurt nodded and they set off. Charles prayed they wouldn't meet anyone, as they must present a grotesque picture and he had no wish to be drawn into explanations—even false ones. If it became necessary, he would say that his friend had had an accident and he himself had sustained injury while trying to rescue him.

Fortunately, they ran into no one and it was almost dark by the time they reached the car.

'We'll drive straight back to the cottage and I'll phone Wragg from there,' Charles said as he headed towards Horsham.

'They meant to kill me,' Kurt said suddenly, speaking for the first time since they'd left the scene of their attack.

'What exactly happened?' Charles asked.

'He gave me a judo attack from behind and try to strangle me. But I learn judo too and break his hold. Then the two of them attack me with fists and kicks, but something frighten them and they suddenly run away. I think it is two people on horse. I try to call to them, but they do

53

not hear and the next thing you are there. One man attack you and one attack me. Then both attack me.'

'Would you be able to recognise them again?'

Kurt shook his head. 'They wear some things over their heads.'

'Did you hear them speak?'

'They speak not much, but they are not English.'

'What were they?'

'Not German.'

'What then?'

Kurt shrugged. 'Perhaps they pretend to be German or Russian—.'

His voice tailed away and he became sunk in thought.

The next few miles passed in silence, which suited Charles who had no particular desire to talk and preferred to try and unravel some of the implications of what had happened before Wragg arrived on the scene.

His thoughts were, however, suddenly interrupted by Kurt who said:

'I must tell you something now, Charles. You ask me before all this happened why such an unimportant person should have fear of being killed. I say that I explain later and I ask you to trust me. You are my friend and you do trust me, but now I will explain.

'They want to kill me because I work in the Ministry of Internal Affairs. It was I who should prevent the others from defecting, but instead I defect myself which makes them very angry. I must be punished "*pour encourager les autres*".' He paused and turned his puffy, blood-stained face towards Charles. 'Now you understand?' The words came as a plea.

'Do you mean you're a member of the secret police?' Charles asked, rather in the tone of one querying a case of venereal disease.

'No, not secret police! I am a civil servant.'

'Have you told Wragg your true role with the delegation?'

'No. I like you to, Charles. Please will *you* tell him.'

'Why can't you tell him? Or more important why haven't you already told him?'

'I think perhaps he know.'

Charles pondered a moment. He'd had occasion already to be impressed by Wragg's omniscience, so what more likely than that Wragg should have known of Kurt's real position in the delegation?

As if in answer to his question, Kurt went on, 'I do not know how much you understand these things, Charles, but every party of visitors from countries in East Europe is watched over by an official.' He gave a small shiver. 'Your authorities know that. It is their job, too, to find out which one is the official. There are ways of discovering. No one is fooled. So this Wragg, he know my position from his other information. But he is so unsimpatico that I do not tell him.' He put a hand up to his face. 'Now perhaps he believe that I am a truthful fugitive.'

Kurt seemed to be saying with teutonic tautology that each country's security service made it its business to know what another's was up to. And this Charles didn't doubt. The whole business of spying and counter-spying seemed to be summed up in the jingle he'd known as a child. 'Big fleas have little fleas upon their backs to bite 'em, little fleas have lesser fleas and so ad infinitum.'

Almost as soon as the car pulled up outside the gate of the cottage, the front-door opened and Sarah stood silhouetted against the light.

'I thought you must be lost or something,' she called out as they came up the path. Then catching sight of Kurt's face, she gave a gasp. 'Good God! What on earth's happened? And you, daddy, you're hurt as well—.'

'We were attacked by two men up on the Downs,' Charles said. 'They tried to kill Kurt, but were content to render me unconscious.'

'I'll phone the doctor,' Sarah said quickly.

'Let me phone Wragg first,' her father said. 'And while I'm doing that you can take Kurt up to the bathroom and help him clean up his face.'

For a second, it looked as though Sarah was going to argue, but then she took Kurt's hand and led him upstairs.

Charles got through to Wragg in a matter of seconds. He explained briefly what had happened and Wragg said he'd drive over immediately and bring a doctor with him. He reacted to the news with neither surprise nor sympathy, and Charles wondered whether he ever showed any emotion beneath his graven exterior.

He arrived in slightly under half an hour and introduced Dr. Mendip, a tall, thin, professional-looking man with a lick of hair falling across his forehead.

'Kurt is lying down upstairs,' Charles explained.

'Take a look at you first then, shall I?' the doctor said and proceeded to examine Charles with gentle expert fingers, while Wragg stood watching.

'Throat uncomfortable?' he asked at one point.

'Yes.'

'From what you've said, your assailant must have been quite a judo expert. Knew just the right amount of pressure to exert to render you unconscious without killing you. Though there are always risks playing around with people's necks,' he added cheerfully. 'I won't let anyone touch mine, not even in fun. Never know with the vagus nerve. It can react unpredictably and then it's too late to be sorry. Death by vagal inhibition, 'spect you've heard of it? Anyway, you've suffered no lasting harm. Your throat'll be sore for a day or two and you have quite a lot of small haemorrhages in both eyes, but they'll disperse quite rapidly. The marks on your neck will be the last to go. If you're embarrassed, you could wear a scarf and pretend you've got a bad throat.' He chuckled. 'Well, you have, haven't you? Anyway, I'll leave you some tablets. Now, I'd better go and see the other chap . . .'

After the doctor had left the room, Charles fetched himself a stiff whisky and prepared to give Wragg a detailed account of what had happened. Wragg declined a drink and sat upright on the edge of his chair as he listened without interruption until Charles finished.

'Had you seen anyone in the vicinity prior to the attack?'

'No. As far as I could see, we had the place to ourselves.'

'And you caught no glimpse of your attackers?'

'None. I only know that the chap who seized me had the grip of a steel vice.'

'A judo expert from all accounts.'

'Kurt, who knows judo, said so.'

'Hm!' The sound seemed to impart Wragg's scepticism of the world and all its works. 'Did Menke talk much while you were out?' he asked a little later.

'Yes, he did. At the beginning he expressed a good deal of disenchantment with the way he was being treated.'

'By me?'

'He seemed fed up with all your questions.'

'I don't know what else he expected! It's like people who get all shirty when Customs go through their bags. I've no patience with them. Anyway, what else did he talk about?'

'He asked me some questions about the Ragnold case.'

'Ah! He did?'

'They were fairly general and he changed the subject when I challenged his interest.' ....

'I'd like you to tell me exactly what he asked and exactly what you told him.'

Charles recounted the conversation in detail, at the end of which Wragg said, 'Hmm!' again.

'There is one other thing I should tell you,' Charles said, after a pause. 'Indeed, Kurt expressly asked me to tell you.' Wragg was watching him with an expression of concentrated wariness. 'He's an official in the East German Ministry of Internal Affairs. He was the man in the delegation who was supposed to keep an eye on the others.' Not by the flicker of a facial muscle, did Wragg show any reaction. 'He says that's why they'll kill him if they get the chance.'

'When did he tell you this?'

'On the way back in the car after we'd been attacked.'

'And he asked you to tell me this?'

'Yes. He said you knew anyway. It was your job to know things like that and you'd have found out.'

To a camera, Wragg's expression would have remained the same, but something in his eyes told Charles that he was, indeed, telling him what he already knew.

'Can you think of anything else that passed between you?'

'No, I think I've told you everything.'

'Depending on what the doctor says, I'll take Menke back to where we're looking after him.' He stared into the ashes of the now almost burnt-out log-fire. 'I certainly never expected anything like that to happen this afternoon,' he said, after a pause. His tone sounded actually worried, so that Charles glanced at him in surprise. It was not that he believed Wragg had organized the assault on them, but he felt sure it must fit in with his overall knowledge of what was going on. But it now appeared not to be so.

Dr. Mendip's voice could be heard at the top of the stairs and a couple of seconds later, he came into the room. He smiled at Charles and went over to speak to Wragg in a lowered tone. Charles decided it was a good moment to go up and see Kurt.

He found him lying comfortably on top of the spare-room bed. Sarah was sitting on the edge and he was clasping her hand.

Now that his face had been cleaned, the full extent of his injuries could be seen. He had numerous small cuts on his face and one large one which ran from the corner of his mouth. This had already been sutured. With the removal of the blood, he looked a much less grim sight than Charles had expected.

'You have told Wragg what I tell you?' he enquired anxiously. The cut, which had widened his mouth, obviously made speech an uncomfortable exercise and his voice sounded as though he was holding a mouthful of liquid.

'Yes, I've told him, but I believe he did know already.'

Kurt gave a satisfied nod. 'That is good. It is easier now.' He smiled at Sarah. 'She is a fine nurse, Charles.'

There were footsteps on the stairs and Wragg appeared in the doorway. For a long time he stared at Kurt in silence in the way you study a picture that catches your interest. Kurt stared back with an expression of quiet defiance.

'The doctor doesn't think you've suffered any worse injuries than are apparent, but he would like some x-rays taken to be on the safe side,' Wragg said, breaking the silence which had threatened to become oppressive. 'He's phoning the hospital now and we'll call in there on the way back.'

He glanced at Sarah. 'Are you Miss Ashmore?'

'I'm sorry, I forgot you hadn't met,' Charles murmured.

Sarah who was still sitting on the bed, her hand in Kurt's, acknowledged the introduction with the briefest of nods.

Ten minutes later, Wragg and the doctor had departed, taking Kurt with them. As they were leaving, Kurt had rested a hand on Charles' arm.

'I am sorry, Charles, that I bring you so much trouble. And with this one'—he made a gesture at Wragg who had his back towards them—'it is not yet over.'

Charles had watched them disappear into the darkness with a sense of foreboding which was proof against even Sarah's company, for she, too, seemed strangely preoccupied that evening.

CHAPTER IX

'IT is important that we talk tonight,' Wragg said when they arrived back at the farmhouse.

'Tomorrow,' Kurt replied petulantly. 'I am tired. I must rest. We talk tomorrow.'

'I'm afraid it must be tonight. There are various matters to be straightened out and they can't wait.'

He led the way into the long, low-ceilinged living-room and went across to switch on the electric fire.

'It is too cold to sit in this room,' Kurt said, hovering in the doorway.

'It'll soon warm up. Would you like a drink? Some brandy might do you good.'

'No. I just need rest.'

'Who were the two men who attacked you?' Wragg asked, ignoring Kurt's mood.

'I have said I do not know. Their faces were covered.'

'But you heard their voices?'

'They do not say much.'

'Do you think they were British or foreign?'

'Perhaps foreign.'

'Why?'

'Why should any British want to kill me?'

'They could have been hired killers. It has happened before.'

Kurt gave a shiver. 'I am nowhere safe.'

'You will be much safer if you tell us the truth. If you want us to help you, you must help us. And keeping things back is not being helpful. Why didn't you admit straight-away that you're a member of one of your security services.'

'Because I believe you know already,' Kurt said testily. 'We all fill in many forms before we come to England. The British intelligence authorities have seen these forms. It is so. They find out who each man is. You know it. I know it. At first when I run away, I am upset. I do not trust anyone. That is why I do not tell you everything, but I know you find out. It is clear from the way you treat me that you know more about me. I merit the big interrogation so you must think I am important. Is it not so, my friend? But the truth from my own lips confirms only what you know.'

'I suggest that you now tell me the *whole* truth,' Wragg said slowly after a long pause.

'What *whole* truth?'

'I want to know every detail of the department you work in. The names of all your colleagues, the addresses, the tele-phone number, the number of windows in your room, which way they face, *everything*.'

'And then you will check and find out what you already know,' Kurt burst out.

'Forget what I'm supposed to know!'

'Ach, I am so tired of this nonsense! Why do you not just leave me alone or send me back to Germany! We go round always in circles. I risk my life to fly from my country and seek freedom in England and all I get is questions. And now someone try to kill me, too. Perhaps it is better in the Deutsche Demokratische Republik and I was a fool to leave. Perhaps, I decide to return—if English freedom permits,' he added in a tone of heavy sarcasm.

Wragg had watched him dispassionately during this outburst. When it finished, he said, 'And now shall we begin?'

CHAPTER X

IF there was one thing which Bowyer's head of section disliked more than any other, it was a meeting first thing on Monday morning. He had an aversion to Mondays and liked to ease himself into the working week.

To make matters worse on this particular Monday, he arrived at his office soaked by rain and uncomfortably aware of a hole in one of his shoes. His arrival coincided with that of Jerome Bowyer who looked annoyingly cheerful and who was wearing his idiotic battered leather hat with its narrow brim turned down all round, making it look like a cross between a child's sou'wester and something out of 'The Boy Friend'.

'They'll be here in a quarter of an hour,' Bowyer said as they parted company at the lift.

'Who's coming?' head of section asked sourly.

'Brigstock and Wragg.'

'That all?'

'Who elso do you suggest?'

'I don't suggest anyone. I was just asking.'

He stumped off to his room, trying to hold himself inside his clothes so that they didn't actually touch him. What a way to start the week! Moreover, he was the one who was going to have to make the actual decisions and carry the responsibility for them thereafter.

Twenty minutes later, the four men were seated round the conference table which head of section had at one end of his room. He himself sat at the head of the table with Bowyer on his right and Brigstock and Wragg on his left. He gave Brigstock a covert glance of distaste as the latter got his pipe going midst clouds of smoke. In a moment, thought head of section, he'll start scratching.

'Probably be best if Wragg sets the ball rolling by bringing us up to date on Menke,' Brigstock said.

Head of section frowned. It seemed he wasn't even allowed to chair a meeting in his own room. 'I was about to propose that course,' he said coldly. He turned to Bowyer. 'I wonder, Jerome, if you would mind not tilting your chair back on its legs like that. You've already been the cause of one falling apart.'

Bowyer assumed an expression of mock penitence and raised his outstretched legs so that the chair fell forward into an upright position. Pulling his hands out of his trouser pockets, he began playing with a paperclip. He knew this would also irritate head of section, which served him right for being so fussy about his silly chairs. It wasn't even as if they were his own; or of any intrinsic value. Just government issue to near top civil servants, which no self-respecting person would allow near his own home.

'Yes, Wragg, go ahead,' head of section said, studiously ignoring Bowyer's casual manipulation of the paperclip.

'Well, as you will know, Menke was yesterday attacked by unknown persons when up on the Sussex Downs with Ashmore, the solicitor with whom he made initial contact when he defected. Ashmore, incidentally, was also attacked and left unconscious. Though neither of them suffered any lasting injuries, they were genuine in the sense that they could not have been self-inflicted. That is to say, even if Menke was Ashmore's attacker, he could not then have inflicted on himself the injuries which he sustained. That is Dr. Mendip's firm view. I may add that I am also satisfied the injuries were caused by others. The question, of course, is who?'

'If Menke works for the K.G.B.,' Brigstock said, removing his pipe and dispersing the smoke which shrouded his face with a wave of his hand, 'it's logical to suppose that it's they who are after his blood.'

'Who knew that Menke was going to spend the day with Ashmore?' Bowyer asked, giving Wragg a nasty little smile.

'Myself and three others in the section. And Tom Brigstock, of course.'

'And Ashmore, of course?'

'Of course.'

'And who did Ashmore tell?'

'His daughter, I imagine.'

'Ahh!'

Wragg flushed. 'I've no reason to believe there's been a leak there.'

'You've no reason not to, either, I presume,' Bowyer said, broadening his smile.

'I imagine it's possible,' head of section said, 'that they've been shadowing him all the time. "Lakeside" may be a secret hideout so far as the man in the street here is concerned, but I bet the K.G.B. know about it.'

'I don't know if you're suggesting that *our* security is lax,' Brigstock said, scratching vigorously just above his right ear.

'My dear fellow, I'm not reproaching anyone,' head of section said loftily, 'but we all know it becomes harder all the time to keep a secret in this business from our fellow pros on the other side.'

'Could Menke himself have communicated with anyone outside?' Bowyer asked.

Wragg shook his head. 'Not while he's been in our care.'

'I incline to agree with you, Brigstock,' head of section said. 'Namely that these were probably K.G.B. boys who carried out the attack. When I say K.G.B., I'm including anyone they may have hired for the afternoon. I take it all the Embassy folk who went out for a Sunday afternoon spin are accounted for?'

'Yes, we checked on that immediately,' Brigstock said. 'But as we all know, the odds favour their getting away with it even when they break bounds.'

'If it was a genuine attack, why didn't they finish off the job and kill Menke?' Bowyer asked.

'They were frightened off,' Wragg replied.

'You've only his word for that.'

'And of course he surprised them by his resistance,'

Wragg added. 'If he hadn't known judo, he almost certainly would have been killed.'

'So he would have us believe.'

'If Menke is telling the truth,' Brigstock said, peering hard at Bowyer through his smokescreen, 'then he is a genuine defector and your agent in East Berlin has led us astray——'

'*If*,' Bowyer said scornfully. 'V has never let us down yet.'

'There has to be a first time even for double agents,' Brigstock said.

'Look,' Bowyer said, in a spurt of exasperation, 'let's leave V out of it for the moment. We'll discuss him a little later on. What I'd like to ask Wragg is, whether he is satisfied that Menke is a phony? Or does he add up to a genuine article after all his interrogation of him?'

Wragg appeared unmoved by Bowyer's veiled attack. Thrusting out his lower lip, he appeared to be giving judicial consideration to his answer.

'When Menke first defected, we believed he was a plant. We believed that simply because your agent V had warned us that a defection was to take place, though he couldn't tell us the object of the particular exercise. In all the hours I have spent with Menke during the past few days, I have not let on that we knew anything about him, and he, for his part, has steadfastly affected the role of an ordinary hygiene official. That is, until yesterday when he informed Ashmore that he was really an intelligence officer in the East German Ministry of Internal Affairs. Which is not the same as working for the K.G.B.,' Wragg added with a meaningful look at Bowyer. 'His reason for not having disclosed this in the first instance and for not informing me in person in the second is in my memo which you have in front of you.'

'Surely nobody believes he didn't disclose his true identity simply because of the initial trauma of defection?' Bowyer asked incredulously.

'I know!' Brigstock said. 'But against that, you have this serious assault on him yesterday.'

'I don't accept that at its face value,' Bowyer said defiantly.

'If he's a plant,' Wragg went on, 'we're still no nearer finding out why.'

'Back to V,' head of section said wearily. 'We always come back to V.' He glanced at Bowyer, who was trying to bend the paperclip back into shape.

'I can't believe that Menke's defection and the Ragnold trial are a pure coincidence. I believe Menke timed his defection because he knew Ashmore was involved in the case, and *that* is where his real interest lies.'

'It's only theorizing,' Brigstock said. 'I'm not saying you're wrong, but there's no evidence to support your idea.'

'Why can't you let Menke slip his lead and see what happens?' Bowyer asked eagerly. 'Pretend not to be watching him and see what he gets up to?'

Wragg looked dubious, but Brigstock said, 'There are risks—for example he might actually be able to shake off surveillance—but I think we might consider it. It's expensive in manpower, but presumably it would only be for a day.'

'Possibly less,' Bowyer said.

'I have a suggestion that I'd like to make,' Wragg said, breaking a short silence, and fixing Bowyer with a hard look. 'I think that direct contact ought to be made with V as a matter of great urgency. Otherwise I foresee the days dragging into a week and longer before we get any information from him by your normal channels of communication. And until V has cleared the air, we're stymied. All we can do is keep Menke on ice and go over and over the same old ground.

'I entirely agree,' Bowyer said, nodding heartily: so much so, in fact, that Wragg's expression became one of suspicion. 'No, I mean it,' he added with an amused look. 'I'd been going to propose the self-same thing. I think I should leave for Berlin today and get in touch with him during the next twenty-four hours.'

All eyes went towards head of section who was sitting with the corners of his mouth turned down and looking a picture of melancholy. 'It would have to be approved higher up,' he said defensively. 'And I'm not sure the end justifies the risks. After all, the odds are we shall get what we want to know from V in the course of the next day or so without recourse to dramatics.'

'But supposing we don't,' Brigstock said. 'It'll be that much more time lost.'

'Also,' Wragg put in, 'it'll give you an opportunity of checking on the chap, of satisfying yourselves that he's not feeding you false information.'

'I don't know why it should be suggested that he is!' head of section said with the natural petulance of one aware that he was being out-manoeuvred.

'I'm in no doubt that V is what he has always been,' Bowyer said energetically, 'namely a bloody good agent in a vital position. But I agree that time is of the essence and. that direct contact is called for. And I'm the obvious man for the job. V is my boy.'

'It still seems to me very odd,' Brigstock said, 'that he was able to tell us of Menke's impending defection, but unable to provide any reason for it. Even to speculate as to a reason. I confess it leaves me with an uneasy feeling about your Mr. —'

'Yes, well, I don't think we need canvass our various doubts all over again,' head of section said testily. 'Is there anything further for discussion at this meeting?'

Everyone shook their heads and Bowyer gave Wragg a broad wink, which said 'leave it to me, I'll overcome the old sod's scruples'.

After Brigstock and Wragg had departed, head of section said accusingly, 'I suppose you'd been planning that all along?'

'I certainly had it in mind,' Bowyer admitted cheerfully, without mentioning that he'd even contemplated it as an unofficial exercise. 'I'm sure it's the only way of breaking the deadlock. We've got to find out why Menke's here and only V can tell us.'

'Well, why hasn't he?'

Bowyer frowned. 'I wouldn't admit it to that couple, but I'm puzzled, too, about that. Indeed, there are a number of points which puzzle me. There are probably simple explanations—there usually are—but it needs someone to go forth and find them. Incidentally, I don't want any of our Berlin people told I'm coming.'

'That'd be most irregular,' head of section said sternly.

'It'll also be much safer.'

'But you may need their help.'

'If I do, I'll yell.'

'You know they don't like being by-passed in matters of this sort. And it's not fair to keep them in the dark.'

'Forget protocol and the proper channels for once.' He glanced at his watch. 'I'll get a plane this afternoon.'

'Your journey hasn't yet received formal approval,' head of section said in a frosty tone as he turned towards the door.

Jerome Bowyer grinned at his reproachful back.

CHAPTER XI

ONLY force of habit and a fastidiousness about his personal appearance induced Kurt Menke to shave the next morning. It was a slow and painful business avoiding the abrasions on his face, but he felt the better when he had finished.

He came down to breakfast to find a stranger in the dining-room. He was younger than Wragg with a curiously impersonal air about him. He was sitting at the unlaid end of the table with a newspaper open before him.

'I'm afraid Mr. Wragg has had to go up to London. My name's Hyde. How are you feeling this morning?'

The three sentences came out without pause as though they were being read from a phrase book.

Kurt brought his heels together and gave the newcomer a small, formal bow. 'Menke,' he said, as though Hyde might be unaware of his name.

'Your face doesn't look too bad,' Hyde said. 'From all accounts I expected to see something worse. Anyway, Dr. Mendip will be here shortly.'

'I am already better, thank you,' Kurt said. 'When will Mr. Wragg return?'

'He's likely to be away all day. Most probably he'll be back about dinner time.'

67

'And so what do I do today?' Kurt enquired in the tone of a child expecting to be amused.

'We thought you'd probably want to rest. As you know, we've got quite a good library here with quite a few German books. We can play cards if you like. Do you play poker?'

'No.'

'I'm not a particularly good chess-player, but I'm happy to have a game with you if you'd like that. Later in the day, there's T.V. to watch. I don't think we'll have much difficulty in making the time pass, but if you have any suggestions, let's hear them.'

Kurt went across to the window and gazed out. The sun was shining and great white clouds were sailing majestically across the sky. The two alsatian guard dogs were chasing scents about the garden in a display of purposeful energy. Kurt didn't like the dogs and reciprocated their suspicion.

'We can go out?' he asked, turning and looking in Hyde's direction.

'Go for a walk, you mean? Yes certainly. It's a perfect day for a walk, though we'll stay clear of the Downs after what happened yesterday.'

'Perhaps we go to London and you show me things?'

'I don't think that's a very good idea,' Hyde said firmly. 'After all, if anyone really is out to kill you, you're much safer here than you would be in London.'

'I would not be safe with you?' Kurt asked with a note of incredulity.

'Protection is always much more difficult to achieve in crowds than somewhere like this.'

Kurt sat down and began his breakfast, at the same time radiating an aura of displeasure. Hyde gave up trying to make further conversation and resumed his reading of the paper with an air of calculated unconcern.

Soon after Kurt had finished, Dr. Mendip arrived and they went up to Kurt's bedroom where the doctor gave him a thorough examination interspersed with brief comments on his patient's condition. When he had finished, he said:

'The cuts'll take a little time to heal, but otherwise I'm glad to report you'll be none the worse for your experience.

The x-rays confirm that you didn't suffer any fractures and all I need do is leave you a prescription for some tablets. I gave you an anti-tetanus injection last night so there's not much danger of any infection.'

Hyde was hovering in the hall when they came back downstairs. After the doctor had departed, he said to Kurt, 'It'll be all right to go to London if you're really very keen on it. I spoke to my superiors while you were upstairs and they said we could.'

'That is good,' Kurt said. 'This place, it is like a prison. You will take me to London and show me the sights, hien?'

'What do you particularly wish to see?'

'I have seen Tower of London and Westminster Abbey and the Buckingham Palace. I like to drive and look at the streets and the people and go into one of the big stores. We do that, yes?'

'All right.'

'When do we leave?'

'As soon as you're ready.'

Kurt beamed. 'I am now ready.'

The journey into London took just under an hour and for the following forty-five minutes they drove around the West End with Hyde, a not particularly communicative guide, pointing out an occasional building and Kurt sitting contentedly at his side gazing out at the constantly changing scene.

At half past twelve, Hyde suggested that they have lunch and they drove to a Greek restaurant in Soho where he was obviously well known. When the meal was over, he excused himself saying he had a phone call to make.

He was away for nearly a quarter of an hour and when he got back to the table, it was to find that Kurt had disappeared.

He sat down but almost immediately got up and went to the gentlemen's toilet to see if Kurt were there. It was no larger than a hen-coop and the merest glance was sufficient to tell him it was empty.

On returning to the table, he motioned over the head-waiter.

'Did you see where my friend went?' he asked.

69

The head-waiter looked blank. 'I enquire, sir. I did not see him leave myself. I ask your waiter.'

He returned a couple of minutes later to explain that Kurt had suddenly manifested signs of agitation, had muttered something about being watched and had made a precipitate exit.

'I expect he's gone to the car,' Hyde said unconcernedly.

After paying the bill, he returned to the telephone booth and made another, but much shorter call.

* * * * *

The young man who had been industriously studying the wares in the porno shop next to the restaurant saw Kurt leave and set off after him at a discreet distance.

The young man's name was Philip de Bercy, which was almost the only fancy thing about him, as he was otherwise the most inconspicuously and commonplace looking person imaginable. This was his great strength as a tail, apart from his natural skill at the job. On this occasion he was dressed in a pair of jeans and an anorak and had put on a pair of spectacles to enhance his student appearance. A duffel bag was slung over one shoulder. On other occasions he had looked equally at home as a gas fitter, a window cleaner and even a bus inspector, all of which were useful disguises when keeping observation on places or people.

For a hundred yards or so, Kurt hurried along with frequent glances over his shoulder. But he was obviously only wanting to make sure that Hyde was not following him. He certainly had no eyes for Philip de Bercy who was loping along on the opposite pavement.

Once he was a safe distance from the restaurant, his pace slackened though he still moved with a sense of purpose. It was apparent that he knew exactly where he wanted to go.

On reaching Cambridge Circus, he hailed a taxi and got in. As he did so, another taxi slid alongside de Bercy and he entered it. The driver didn't require any instructions, but set off after the first taxi, which was heading towards Oxford Street. When it got there, it turned right to travel east.

'Any idea where he's off to?' the driver of Philip de Bercy's taxi asked.

'Nope.' A little later, however, he said, 'It could be the Old Bailey. We'll soon know.'

'Yes, it is the Old Bailey,' the driver said as the taxi ahead of them swung right and drew up in front of the main entrance. 'You'd better get out here and I'll park this side.' He turned his head and grinned. 'Forgot to switch off the "For Hire" sign the other day. Got a very dirty look when I refused to be flagged down. And an earful of abuse!'

Philip de Bercy got out and saw Kurt examining the Court lists which were on the wall just beside the main entrance. There was clearly only one case in which he could have any interest—and that was going on in Court 1.

After a couple of minutes, Kurt went up the steps into the building and de Bercy crossed the road and followed him in.

Kurt spoke to a uniformed officer on duty outside the entrance to Court 1 and was apparently given instructions to the public gallery.

De Bercy waited for three or four minutes before entering the gallery himself. Kurt had squeezed himself on to the end of a seat in the front row. De Bercy took one at the back near the door.

The police officer on duty in the public gallery gave him a long, appraising look and he was glad he had left his duffel bag in the taxi. Almost certainly he wouldn't have been allowed to take it into Court and anything that led to wrangles or confrontations was always to be studiously avoided. He later noticed that everyone entering the gallery was subjected to the same long, hard stare from the officer.

Kurt was sitting forward, gazing intently at the scene below, which lay like a tableau before their eyes. Its centre-piece was Evelyn Ragnold sitting quietly in the spacious dock, his hands folded in his lap.

Once or twice he glanced up at the public gallery and de Bercy watched him expectantly, but he gave no sign of recognising anyone—or, indeed, a sign of anything.

It wasn't part of his business—at his junior level in the security service, your life was strictly compartmentalized— but he couldn't help speculating on the reason for Menke's visit to the Court where Ragnold was on trial.

71

He had been warned that once Menke thought he'd slipped his lead it was one of the places he might make for and so it had proved to be.

De Bercy's instructions were simply to tail him and make a full report on everywhere he went and everything he did. Well, unless he was practising telepathy, his visit to the Old Bailey seemed to be that of a passive spectator. And yet this was just what it shouldn't be from all de Bercy had gathered!

He suddenly stiffened as he observed Menke lean forward as though to peer over the front edge of the gallery. He appeared to be fumbling with his hands. The next moment he had risen and hurried up the steps to the door at the back, while two or three people in the front row turned and stared after him in surprise.

De Bercy had no time to discover what had happened before hurrying off after his quarry. He caught up with him in the main hall of the building and followed him out into the road where he made a bee-line for a public call-box. De Bercy watched him go inside and dial a number. He appeared to do so without reference to any piece of paper, so it was clearly one he knew.

When Menke came out of the kiosk after a conversation lasting only seconds, he hailed a passing taxi. De Bercy stepped into his own tame one which had drawn up at his side while Menke was making his phone call and they set off behind the other.

'He didn't spend long in there,' the driver said conversationally as he kept a comfortable twenty yards behind the taxi ahead.

'Do you mean in the call box?'

'No, at the Old Bailey.'

'He did something funny just as he was about to leave and I don't know what it was,' de Bercy said in a worried tone. 'I didn't have time to stop and find out.'

'What sort of a funny thing?'

'I don't know. As if he was tossing something down into the Court.'

'At least it couldn't have been a bomb!'

De Bercy grunted. 'Look, he's getting out!'

They saw Kurt pay off the cab and cross the pavement to

a doorway where he paused to examine the name-plate. A moment later, he entered the building.

De Bercy waited a few seconds before following him. He, too, paused at the door: *Quigley, Smith & Co., Solicitors and Commissioners for Oaths,* he read.

CHAPTER XII

To Charles Ashmore, the atmosphere of Number One Court at the Old Bailey became increasingly claustrophobic and oppressive as the trial proceeded. Today had been particularly bad, though he was prepared to accept—or, rather, he attempted to persuade himself—that the traumas of the previous day were largely responsible. After all, it wasn't every day that he was attacked and left unconscious beneath a beech tree.

Nevertheless, he was unable to recall a case which he had found so distasteful. Though this again was perhaps not so surprising. In the first place, he scarcely ever went into the criminal courts and to do so on behalf of an army officer charged with spying could never be an enjoyable experience.

He had reached a stage, however, where he had become almost detached. Whatever verdict was returned against his enigmatic client would find him unmoved. He realized that his mood had been subconsciously induced by his feeling of repugnance, but it had now settled on him like a pall.

The afternoon session had not advanced very far when he became aware that those facing him across the table in the well of the Court were staring up at the public gallery. Charles turned his head, but was unable to see what had caused the sudden flutter of interest. He noticed that a woman sitting two rows behind Counsel and on a level with the front of the dock had an affronted expression and was anxiously fingering her hat. For a moment he wondered if a bird had got into Court.

By the time he turned back again, interest in whatever had happened appeared to have evaporated, save that one of the Special Branch officers had slipped out of his seat and tiptoed round to where the woman was sitting.

Eventually the Court rose for the day and Charles gathered his papers together and put them into his briefcase. When he turned round to speak to Counsel, he saw that Ainsworth, his leader, was talking to Counsel for the Prosecution. Their conversation ended and Ainsworth returned.

'I gather someone in the public gallery threw down a piece of paper which has considerably excited our friends in the security service,' Ainsworth said, with a dry smile.

'Is that what all the staring was about?' Charles said.

'Apparently. I didn't notice anything myself.'

'Why should that have caused the security people so much interest?'

'They think it was aimed at our chap in the dock.'

'Seems a fairly primitive method of communication. Anyway, what was written on the piece of paper?'

'Ah! That's a dark secret. Nobody's been told. For all I know, it may even have been a blank piece.'

'Who's supposed to have thrown it?'

'No one seems to know. I gather he hurried out and disappeared immediately afterwards.'

'Why do they think it was aimed at Ragnold?'

'Well, they seem to think it was done deliberately and, once you accept that premise, I suppose the man in the dock becomes the most likely target. It clearly wasn't intended for the lady on whose hat it landed. And, when you come to think of it, there is only one person in this Court beyond the reach of normal communication. Namely, Ragnold.'

Charles looked pensive. 'Well, I hope they don't suspect his legal advisers of complicity in such nonsense,' he said after a pause.

'Suspicious lot that they are, I'm sure they don't suspect that,' Ainsworth said with a look of amusement. 'However, it might be as well to have a word with Ragnold when you go down to the cells. Mention it to him and see what his reaction is.'

'I will. Incidentally, I'd better get down there now or they'll be whipping him back to Brixton for the night.'

Evelyn Ragnold was sipping a cup of tea when Charles entered the cell. 'Gets very stuffy in Court by the end of the day,' he remarked in a deprecating tone. 'I'm sure the chief officer could get you a cup, too, if you like.'

'No thanks, I'll wait till I get back to my office.'

'You're probably wise. This is rather like army tea, thick and sweet and strong enough to line your whole stomach with tannin.'

'Did you notice that small disturbance in Court this afternoon?' Charles asked in a casual tone.

'You mean the woman who got hit on the head by something thrown from the public gallery?' Charles nodded. 'It didn't seem much of a disturbance to me,' Ragnold said. 'I created a much better one when I was a small boy and an old aunt took me and two cousins to the pantomime one Christmas. We had seats in the front row of the circle and what do I do but topple our box of chocolates over the edge. I think the children in the stalls thought it was part of the show having chocolates rain on them, but the comic who was just about to do his turn didn't think it a bit funny and my two cousins were absolutely livid.'

Charles listened to this reminiscence with a sense of unreality. If Evelyn Ragnold could recount such anecdotes at such a time, he was easily capable of selling State secrets to the highest bidder.

'I gather it was a piece of paper that was thrown,' he said bleakly in the voice of one who feels reluctantly obliged to continue what he has begun.

'I didn't see,' Ragnold said without interest.

'The security people seem to think it might have been a message intended for you.'

Ragnold's eyes opened wide as he stared at Charles. 'What an extraordinary notion! What was the supposed message?'

'That hasn't been disclosed to me.'

'Even if it had been a tip for the three-thirty, it wouldn't have done me much good.'

'Did you happen to notice the chap in the gallery who threw it?'

Ragnold shook his head. 'The only chap I've noticed up there is an elderly man who turns up every day and sits in the same place. I suspect he comes in to get out of the cold.' A smile broke across his face. 'The weather cold, I mean, not the one that spies come in from.'

'Well, that seems to dispose of that,' Charles said in a tone of relief. 'I'll let Counsel know. They thought I ought to get your reaction.'

'It seems a pretty crude means of communication, anyway,' Ragnold said with a thoughtful frown. 'If I'm the cunning chap they seem to believe I am, I'm surprised they think that.' He gave Charles a small, enigmatic smile. 'I feel I've let everyone down by not admitting that I was expecting a mysterious message.'

'I'm glad to know, as I suspected, that there's nothing to it,' Charles said stiffly.

It was only as he was leaving the Old Bailey it occurred to him that Ragnold had never commented on the signs he bore of the recent assault. Perhaps this was a further sign of his client's complete egocentricity. He was interested only in himself.

Anyway, he was glad that Ragnold hadn't commented as he had been forced into explaining that he'd had a fall in the garden. This had been Wragg's suggestion after he had persuaded Charles that it was not a matter for reporting to the police.

Charles had been quite agreeable about not reporting the attack, but he was not a good liar and he had been embarrassed all day by having to give a gratuitously false account to those who kindly enquired what had happened.

He hailed a taxi and gave the driver his office address. He had scarcely arrived and entered the small reception lobby when his secretary, who had clearly been listening intently for his footfall, shot out of her room and came hurrying towards him.

'Oh, Mr. Ashmore,' she said in a breathless whisper, 'There's that Mr. Menke here waiting to see you.'

Charles stopped in his tracks as though he'd walked into an invisible wall. 'Kurt Menke? Here?'

Miss Acres, who had been his secretary for over twenty years, gazed at him anxiously. 'He arrived over an hour ago and insisted upon waiting. He seemed very upset about something. I took the liberty of telling Mr. Quigley and he did go and speak to him.'

Charles grimaced. He had given his senior partner the minimum of details about Kurt's defection and the last thing he wanted was his intrusion on the scene. He had also told about as much to Miss Acres and sworn her to secrecy. She was, in any event, the soul of discretion where her employer's affairs were concerned. On the other hand, Walter Quigley's sense of discretion was as variable as a weather vane where other people's affairs were concerned.

It was at that moment that the firm's senior partner emerged from his office along the corridor.

'Ah! You're back!' he said, advancing towards Charles with a portentous expression. 'I suppose Miss Acres has told you about this fellow Menke bursting in here this afternoon.'

'Yes, I gather he's waiting to see me,' Charles replied.

'I had him put into your office. Didn't want him mixing with clients in the waiting-room!' He seemed to become suddenly aware of the marks on Charles' face. 'What's happened to your face?'

'I had a small accident over the weekend.' For once, the lie came glibly. 'I gather you spoke to Kurt yourself?'

'When Miss Acres very properly told me he was here, I had to do something. I wondered whether I should ring the police, but he promised to sit quietly until you got back, so I decided to leave it.'

'I'll go and see him right away.'

'And you might ask him not to come bursting in here again. It could lead to all manner of embarrassment.'

Charles studiedly ignored the reproach and pushed past Quigley to reach his office which lay on the opposite side of the corridor from his senior partner's.

Kurt who was sitting slumped in a chair leapt up as Charles entered.

'I am here for refuge,' he said dramatically. 'I was feared for my life and luckily I remember your address.'

'But what are you doing in London, anyway?'

While Kurt explained, Charles hung up his coat and went and sat down at his desk. Kurt, however, remained standing as, with a wealth of gesticulation, he told how when Hyde had left him at the table in the restaurant he had become aware of two men watching him from the pavement outside. He became nervous of their intentions and when they moved across to a car on the other side of the road he had fled. He had, he went on, taken a taxi to the Old Bailey, but had been unable to get into Court to speak to Charles and so had taken another taxi to the office.

'You came to the Old Bailey?' Charles asked incredulously.

Kurt nodded energetically. 'The policeman will not let me into the Court and tell me to go upstairs to the public seats. But up there all I can see is the back of your head down below. I try to attract your attention, but it is no good and I leave and come here.' He paused and searched Charles' face for some sign of sympathy. 'I am sorry if I do wrong but I am most afraid. You must understand that.'

'How did you try and attract my attention in Court?' Charles asked.

'I threw a piece of paper, but you do not notice.'

Charles had the greatest difficulty not to burst out laughing. So that was what the afternoon's diversion was all about! And to think he had been the innocent centrepiece! The security people were not going to be amused when they learned the truth, but it served them right for seeing bogies where none existed. They really were too grim and solemn for words!

'The first thing we'd better do,' Charles said, feeling as if a considerable weight had been lifted off his shoulders, 'is phone Wragg. He's probably got half London looking for you by now.'

'His colleague shouldn't have left me in the restaurant,' Kurt said defensively. 'Those men could have captured me, if I had not run away.'

Charles asked their telephonist for a line and dialled the number which Wragg had given him.

'Mr. Wragg? Charles Ashmore here. I have Kurt Menke with me . . . Yes, in my office . . . Right, we'll wait here till you come.'

Charles replaced the receiver. He supposed it was another facet of membership of the security service. Never show surprise to the outside world. It was as though Wragg had been sitting by the phone waiting for his call.

CHAPTER XIII

'ASHMORE'S just phoned to say that Menke's at his office,' Wragg said, putting his head round the door of Brigstock's room.

Brigstock glanced at his watch.

'He's done that in reasonable time.'

'Within twenty minutes of his return.'

'It'll be interesting to learn how much Menke has told Ashmore of his afternoon's adventures.'

'Have we got hold of the piece of paper yet?'

'Yes. I haven't seen it myself, but Carter has it.'

'It must go to the cryptograph people immediately.'

'Of course.'

'What is it—figures or letters?'

'Figures. Four groups.'

Brigstock frowned. 'How the hell could Ragnold have deciphered it? He can't have any decoding equipment in prison!'

'A small sheet of paper would be sufficient, assuming only limited communication was intended.'

'We'd better find out. His cell must be searched when he's out of it tomorrow and the prison people must find an excuse to get hold of his clothing. There may be something sewn into a lining.'

79

'I've already arranged for that,' Wragg said. 'And his cell's being searched before he returns to it tonight.'

Brigstock gave a satisfied grunt. 'Well, it certainly seems to have paid off giving him a bit of rope. I didn't think he'd seize the opportunity quite so crudely.'

'Paid off in one sense, but it's explained nothing.'

'It has gone to confirm that Menke's up to some trickery vis-à-vis Ragnold.'

'Either Menke is genuine or he's a fake. Today's events indicate he's a fake. Yesterday's that he's genuine.'

'Not necessarily,' Brigstock said knocking out his pipe against the edge of his desk and examining the result like a scientific explorer. 'There may be another interested party. Had you thought of that?'

'Such as?'

'A third party with an interest in the shenanigans.'

A silence fell. Then Wragg said, 'Bowyer should be on his way to Berlin by now.'

CHAPTER XIV

JEROME BOWYER glanced at the girl beside him. She was staring at the back of the seat in front of her with a withdrawn air. She had hardly said a word since they had changed planes in Frankfurt.

The Pan Am 727 was packed as planes on the Berlin run usually were. They were flying through cloud at nine thousand feet, which was neither the best height for the plane nor its passengers, but happily it was only a fifty minute hop and in another quarter of an hour they'd be landing at Tempelhof airport in the heart of West Berlin.

Bowyer felt excited as he always did on the eve of action. His adrenalin had been flowing all day and now he was positively aware of it coursing through his veins, though none of this was apparent to a stranger's eye. He turned his head to look again at the girl.

'We'll be landing in a few minutes,' he said, quietly.

She moved her head slightly, but otherwise gave no sign of having heard him.

'You're not sorry you've come?' he whispered.

'No.' Her tone was as far away as her expression.

It wasn't to be wondered at, Bowyer reflected. She was experiencing the inevitable reaction of a quixotic decision made in bizarre circumstances. He realized he hadn't been fair on her, not that that bothered him. His only concern was that she wouldn't now prove to be a liability. After all, his own conduct in pressing her to accompany him had, to say the least, been quixotic, but he refused to believe that his judgement might let him down. Not if she was the same old Sarah he remembered . . .

Sarah had just been having her mid-morning cup of coffee when the phone in her office had rung and a voice had said, 'Remember me, Sarah, it's Jerome?'

'Of course I remember you,' she had replied eagerly, preparing herself for a cosy chat.

'Good, then meet me outside your office in ten minutes. I'll pick you up in a car.'

'I can't possibly do that. But I usually go to lunch at half past twelve and could meet you then.'

'That'll be too late. This is something urgent, Sarah. You know me. I wouldn't say that if it weren't.'

It was at this point she had recalled that Jerome Bowyer was in some way caught up in the Menke affair, which in turn meant in her father's affairs. It must be to do with that matter that he wished to see her. Nevertheless her tone was doubtful when she replied.

'Well, I might be able to slip out for a few minutes.'

She had heard him chuckle—the slightly manic chuckle she remembered so well which had always either scared or exhilarated her. Though that often amounted to the same thing.

'That's great, Sarah. I knew you couldn't have changed. It'll be a treat to see you again.' She had responded to the quaintly expressed sentiment with a small laugh which had frozen in her throat as he went on, 'By the way, better tell your boss you'll be away for a couple of days or so—perhaps for the rest of this week. See you in ten minutes.'

He had rung off, leaving her staring disbelievingly at the instrument which had conveyed such wildly improbable instructions.

Almost as if in a sleepwalk—though a brisk, purposeful sleepwalk—she had gone into her employer's office and said she had been called away suddenly to the bedside of a dying aunt in Wales. Luckily, her boss had always been wholly incurious about her personal life and so had no idea of either the number or the state of health of her aunts. In fact, she had only one, an immensely tough old bird who lived in the highlands of Scotland. He had accepted her imminent departure with a murmur of sympathy and the hope that her aunt wouldn't suffer unnecessarily. He urged her to let him know if there was anything he could do, at the same time making it clear that he wouldn't cry if there wasn't.

As she stepped out on to the pavement, a car drew up and Jerome Bowyer leaned across from the driver's seat to open the passenger door. He might have been picking her up every day of the week for the past twelve months.

'I'll take you straight to your flat so that you can pack a bag,' he said. 'We don't have to be at the airport till two, so we've got a bit of time.'

'You didn't say anything on the phone about catching a plane.'

'It wasn't exactly the moment.'

'Well, tell me now, where are we going?'

'Berlin.' He said it as though the answer were self-evident.

Sarah gazed at him with a mixture of excitement and exasperation.

'You really are the most incredible person! We've not seen each other for years and then you ring me up out of the blue and expect me to join you on some improbable expedition at ten minutes' notice!'

'And here you are!' he said affably.

'God knows why!'

'Because you're the same Sarah who once worked in the

outfit and because you have the same irreverent attitude towards much of the nonsense as I have.'

'Go on. That's not all.'

He grinned in a mildly self-deprecating manner. 'And because, too, you've never completely exorcized me. I can still do something to your chemistry.'

'I can tell you haven't changed either,' she said. 'You're as conceited as you always were.'

'No, I'm not conceited. I'm just a realist where you and I are concerned.'

Half an hour later, Sarah had changed into more suitable clothes for travelling, packed a bag and written a short note to her father saying she'd been sent over to Paris at short notice by her firm but would be back by the weekend. This she dropped through the letter-box of his house on their journey to the airport.

'Isn't it time you told me what this is all about?' she asked as they nosed their way towards the M4 and the ten-mile sprint to Heathrow. 'After all, I've dropped everything to fly to your assistance and I don't even know what's expected of me.'

He put out a hand and patted her knee. 'Don't spoil it by being querulous,' he said with a wry smile. 'You never used to be. Moreover, you wouldn't have agreed to come if you weren't the same old Sarah.'

'I'm getting tired of the "same old Sarah" song, just tell me why you need me to accompany you to Berlin. It's obviously something to do with my father, isn't it?'

'How well do you know Kurt Menke?' His tone was businesslike with an abrupt change of mood.

'I'd never met him until the evening he arrived at daddy's house.'

'But you'd obviously heard your father talk about him?'

'Certainly. After all, they'd known one another for something like thirty-five years. Daddy often used to talk about his year in Berlin when he stayed with the Menkes.' She paused for a moment. 'When I say often, I don't mean he went out of his way to do so, but if the subject of pre-war Germany came up he would usually recall his own experiences there.'

Bowyer looked pensive, but Sarah couldn't tell whether he was concentrating on the traffic or considering what she had said.

'Let me ask you a straight question,' he said, breaking their silence. 'Do you think Kurt Menke is a genuine defector?'

She looked at him sharply. 'The answer to that is simple: I have no reason to doubt him. But you obviously do. Is that why we're going to Berlin?'

'Yes.'

'You don't suspect my father of anything?' she asked in an anxious tone.

'I have no reason to,' he said with a small smile.

'And why do you need me to come along?'

'Our Berlin people don't know I'm coming. I was insistent they shouldn't be told . . .'

'Why?'

'Because I want to conduct this operation my way without interference. And one thing for sure, if they knew I was coming they'd have to stick several fingers in. There'd be arguments, alterations, recriminations and, in all, a bloody waste of time leading to a likely cock-up. Our Berlin section is full of fine fellows, but it's always been a station which has bred rivalries and jealousies. It's inevitable given the set-up there. Ater a quarter of a century, it's still pre-eminently a hotbed of spies but I don't intend to get caught up with any of their machinations on this trip.'

'And where's my place in this one-man operation?'

'I must have one person whom I can trust; one person in the trenches with me.'

'Doing exactly what?'

'That's what I don't know at the moment. It'll depend on the results of a preliminary reconnaissance. I shall cross into East Berlin this evening and have a scout around and make my plans in the light of what I discover then.'

'Shall I be accompanying you?'

'No. I shall leave you warm and snug with a bottle of wine and a T.V. set.'

Sarah looked thoughtful for a few seconds.

'Where'll we be staying?'

'Not in a hotel.'

'It seems I have to take a fair amount on trust.'

'A fair amount, yes.' His tone was gently mocking. 'But you know from your own experience the rules governing the secret Olympics.'

'Do your bosses at home know that I'm accompanying you?'

'Good gracious, no! They'd have kittens all over their office carpets.'

Sarah smiled. 'That I can imagine.'

'If they ever find out, I'll probably be locked up in the Tower, but they won't be able to touch you.'

Sarah snuggled back against the car seat. 'Give me a quick run down on your life since we last met,' she said.

'That's funny!'

'Why?'

'I was just about to say the very same thing to you.'

They had chattered away animatedly throughout the flight from London to Frankfurt, Sarah suddenly finding herself caught up in the excitement of their journey and responding happily to Jerome Bowyer's characteristic bravura.

But on the plane to Berlin, her eager mood seemed to burn itself out and she became silent and withdrawn.

The plane suddenly ducked out of cloud and there below them was a lake, one of those strung along Berlin's western perimeter. Beyond Jerome could see the autobahn stretching into the city's built-up area.

He gazed out intently. The place was making an arcking approach over the north-western suburbs which meant they would be coming into land from the east over the communist sector, for Tempelhof was scarcely a stone's throw from the wall.

The 'no smoking' sign had come on and he slowly re-fastened his seat-belt.

'Only a couple of minutes now,' he said quietly to Sarah as if waking a child from sleep.

She gave an abstracted nod and looked dutifully out of the window.

'That's the new television tower in East Berlin,' he remarked as they both looked at a tall, gleaming structure which was reflecting the last rays of daylight.

'They all looked exactly alike. I can never see why cities are so pleased to have them. They're just great knobbly fingers.'

'That one certainly has a nasty swelling near the tip,' he agreed.

'Doubtless a revolving restaurant. They all have them!'

'I seem to think it is.' He turned his head to observe the tower as it passed to their rear. 'On the whole I'm reasonably impervious to them,' he added, as he sat back in his seat.

'I think they should build them underground!'

It was while he was pondering this that the plane touched down and a minute or two later came to a halt beneath the vast canopy of the terminal building.

'We'll get a taxi,' he said as soon as they had claimed their bags.

He strode through the crowd in the entrance hall with Sarah hurrying to keep up beside him. There was a queue of taxis outside and he thrust her into the first and piled in behind her as though they had suddenly become the objects of pursuit.

He gave the driver rapid instructions in German and they set off.

'Sorry about that,' he said as the taxi turned into the main stream of traffic, 'but you never know who you'll run into at Tempelhof. It's Berlin's eye of the needle. However I didn't see anyone I knew, so the odds are no one saw me.'

'Where are we going now?'

'To a flat in the Hansa quarter, just north of the Tiergarten.'

'Is that far?'

'About fifteen minutes' ride. Maybe twenty.'

'Whose flat is it?'

'Belongs to someone I know.'

'Male or female?'

'Female. But she won't be there.'

'Does she know we're coming?'

'No.'

'Where is she?'

'When I last heard, she was in Bangkok.'

'Oh!'

'Any further questions?'

'Not for the moment.'

'It's a pleasant flat. I think you'll like it. It's in a new block.'

'How big?'

'Two bedrooms.'

'Oh!'

'That answer your question?'

'I just wondered, that's all.'

Sarah stared out of the window at the brightly lit city. The pavements were thronged and the shop windows were such as to beguile anyone other than a miser and everywhere neon lights flashed out their feverish invitations.

'I always like this hour of the day in any city,' he said. 'It has an air of expectancy and allure that none other has.'

'It's just because you associate it with drinking time.'

'Largely, but not entirely.' He leaned towards her and smiled. 'You didn't expect me to agree with you about that, did you? Now be honest and admit it.'

She smiled back. 'I could do with a drink myself.'

'Well, you haven't long to wait,' he said, as the taxi drew up.

Sarah got out and stared at the peeling stucco building which was the colour of school porridge.

'I thought you said it was a new block,' she remarked.

'This isn't it. Our place is round a couple of corners from here, but I didn't want to give the driver our true address.'

Sarah laughed. 'I've got out of practice since I left the service. It would never have occurred to me.'

Jerome Bowyer picked up their bags and said casually, 'By the way, my name's Sean O'Riordan. I'm travelling on an Irish passport under that name.'

'And what about me?'

'You're still just Sarah Ashmore.'

'And what does Mr. O'Riordan do for a living?'

'He's a journalist. He's also fairly anti-British. I'll tell you more about him later if you're interested.' He nodded at an elegant towerblock on their right, and said, 'This is where we're staying.'

The entrance lobby was warm and softly lit with a huge vase of gladioli on a marble table against the side wall. On the opposite side were two lifts, one with doors open as though it had been patiently waiting for them all day.

Bowyer pressed the button for the eighth floor and they rose with the silent power of a projectile. When they stepped out there was only one door in sight. He noticed Sarah looking about her in surprise and said: 'It's the only flat on this floor. It goes all the way round.'

He fished a key out of his pocket and inserted it in the lock. It seemed to Sarah that it was almost as complicated as opening the door of a safe as he then selected another key for a further lock. But it was equally obvious that he had opened this particular door a good many times in the past.

He reached inside and turned on a light and stood aside for Sarah to enter.

'I'll take you on a quick tour,' he said, closing the door behind them. 'It's really rather a stupendous view as it covers every quarter of the city.'

'Rather like being in a revolving restaurant!'

He laughed. 'Yes. There's the T.V. tower.'

'And that's in East Berlin?'

He nodded. 'I suppose it's about a couple of miles from here. The wall is where you can see that line of arc lights shining.'

Sarah gave a small shiver. 'It all looks so quiet and harmless from here. And yet ...'

'As you say: and yet. Come on, I'll show you the rest of the flat. Not that there's all that much.'

The kitchen looked as though it had been lifted straight from a modern exhibition of kitchen ware. The bath was circular and made of green marble and was, Sarah reckoned, large enough to accommodate three.

The first bedroom they looked into was relatively small. Against one wall was a divan bed covered by a white counterpane which looked as though it were made of polar bear skins. A number of brightly coloured cushions lay artfully arranged at one end.

The main bedroom was much larger and was remarkable not only for its opulence, but for the enormous bed which dominated the room. A canopy of purple velvet adorned one end and matched the carpet which was of the same colour.

Sarah had a wild picture of three people sleeping in it and getting up in the morning to troop off and have a bath together.

They returned to the living-room which was as expensively furnished as the rest of the flat.

'Now let's have a drink,' he said, opening a cabinet just inside the door. 'I think I can offer you anything. I know what, let's have champagne! I feel the occasion calls for celebration. I'll go and get a bottle from the kitchen. There's usually one on ice.'

'Your friend certainly leaves everything very shipshape when she goes off to Bangkok,' Sarah observed as, a few minutes later, she sipped her champagne. 'Champagne on ice, food in the refrigerator, beds made. Absolutely nothing overlooked.'

Bowyer grinned. 'Well, she never knows when an Irish friend mayn't drop by and need sustenance.'

He knew that Sarah was longing to know more of the mysterious owner of the flat. He also knew that she would sooner bite off her tongue than ask him leading questions. This was fine as he had no intention of telling her anyway.

He glanced at his watch. 'I'll be going out in about an hour's time. I want you to stay here. You can listen to the radio, play records, watch T.V., read. Anything you like, but don't go out. I shall be back by midnight. O.K.?'

Sarah nodded.

'And one other thing. If the phone rings, don't answer it... Not on any account.'

When they had finished the champagne, he went out of the room and Sarah heard him moving about in the small bedroom.

After a while she got up and went and stood by the window. She didn't hear him come back and jumped when he suddenly materialized at her side. For a time they stood in

89

silence gazing out across the divided city, with its areas of brilliant light interspersed with dark patches.

'How will you get into East Berlin?' she asked with a slight catch in her voice.

'See that electric train weaving along. That's the Stadt-Bahn, the overhead railway. It covers the whole city, east and west in a vast network, but there's only one line left which connects the two halves. In about three minutes' time, that little glow-worm of a train will have burrowed through the wall and arrived at the Friedrichstrasse Station in East Berlin. It's only a couple of stations ride from here.'

The train which had temporarily disappeared came into view again as it curved around the northern perimeter of the Tiergarten, the great park in the heart of Berlin.

'That's the quickest way from here. Or one could go by U-Bahn and also land up at the Friedrichstrasse Station, but that would involve a couple of changes. Or I could take a taxi to Checkpoint Charley and then walk through. But I'll probably go on the S-Bahn.'

'Do you know exactly what you'll be doing when you get there?'

'Exactly.'

As she watched him put on a short suede coat with a fleece lining, she realized it was not a garment he had brought with him, though from the fit, it was clearly his.

At the front door he suddenly kissed her as though it was the most natural thing to do.

For several seconds after he had gone, Sarah felt seized by panic. What on earth was she doing in this strange flat which, for all its opulence, now seemed filled with sinister reminders of her mad journey.

Jerome Bowyer had told her nothing. Nothing! And what did she know about him? Of the real Jerome Bowyer? Precious little. He was as mysterious as the absent owner of the flat. And here she was alone eight floors up in a strange city with no idea why she was there, other than that someone with whom she had once believed herself to be in love had suddenly bobbed into her life again. Bobbed was the word, his features danced before her mind's eye like a face on a Hallowe'en lantern.

Without warning the telephone began to ring and she stared mesmerized at the small white instrument which crouched on the table beside the long wall sofa. It seemed to go on for ever and she found herself wanting to pick it up just to end the awful suspense, whatever the consequences.

And then as abruptly as it had started, it ceased. But for several seconds she continued staring at it as if expecting it to spring once more into venomous life.

Later she fetched herself a large brandy from the well-stocked cabinet and settled down to anaesthetize her mind with the additional assistance of the television set.

CHAPTER XV

IT was half past eight before Charles Ashmore arrived home that evening. It had been one hell of a day and he was tired and dispirited. Coming on top of the physical assault to which he had been subjected the previous day, he felt distinctly older than his fifty-five years, a state which was rare in his case and which occasioned him an added element of resentment.

He saw Sarah's note on the hall table as soon as he closed the front door and picked it up with a feeling of apprehension. Her notes always affected him in the same manner that his parents' generation reacted to telegrams. They imported an air of drama. And drama was the last thing he wanted at this particular moment. Indeed, he had been hoping Sarah would come round so that he could discuss with her the recent Menke developments. He had been going to phone her as soon as he reached home.

He opened the envelope with fingers that trembled slightly. His first reaction to her news was one of relief. There were worse things than being sent over to Paris by your firm, though she had never given any indication that she might be expected to travel in the job. Perhaps she was

91

as surprised as he now was. Anyway, he was glad for her sake if not for his own.

On the way up to his bedroom, he mixed himself a powerful dry martini. He downed the first in two gulps and poured a second which he took with him upstairs.

By the time he had had a shower and changed, he was feeling somewhat better. He liked to think, moreover, that this was as much due to getting out of clothes which he associated with Court and the Ragnold trial as it was to the effects of gin.

And it was Evelyn Ragnold, he recognized, who was the cause of his present malaise. Much more so than Kurt Menke for all his mercurial. behaviour. Perhaps it was because he had a responsibility for Ragnold's ultimate fate which he didn't have for Kurt. But he believed that this was only part of the story. Ragnold was a silent enigma where Kurt was a fire cracker. Witness the way he had launched out at Wragg and the other man, Hyde, when they had arrived at the office of Quigley, Smith & Co. in answer to Charles' call. There'd been nothing humble or apologetic in his manner then. Instead he had accused Hyde of exposing him to danger and of failing to give him the protection to which he was entitled. At one moment it had seemed as if he might burst out with, 'If this is the way England treats an honest defector, she doesn't deserve to have any.'

Admittedly, Wragg had seemed singularly unmoved by all the denunciations and, afterwards, when Hyde and Kurt had left together, he had subjected Charles to one of his machine-like interrogations about the afternoon's events. He had given little away, but had nevertheless, managed to leave Charles wondering just what Kurt was up to.

So far he had had neither the opportunity nor the inclination to probe beneath the surface reason for Kurt's defection. That was the responsibility of the security service. But now he was being inexorably dragged further into l'affaire Menke. Dragged in without knowing what was going on.

Come to think of it, some of Wragg's questions had almost implied that he, Charles Ashmore, was involved in some mysterious way in the various goings-on.

And now to cap everything, Sarah had gone off to Paris

92

just when he most needed her shrewd, if sometimes erratic, observations on a situation which was worrying him. He felt lonely and deserted.

After he had dined, he decided that his mind required the balm of television. It didn't really matter what the programme was as long as his senses were peacefully engaged in chewing the proffered cud.

About eleven o'clock, there was a knock on the drawing-room door and Burden came in.

'I've just found this on the mat, sir.' He handed Charles a letter. 'It must have been delivered by hand, but no one has rung the front-door bell this evening and I've no idea when it came.'

On the front of the cheap buff envelope was typed: 'Mr. Charles Ashmore, 8 Edgeworth Terrace, S.W.3.'

Burden retired from the room and Charles slit open the envelope with the small penknife he carried on his key-ring. Inside on a half-sheet of plain white paper was typewritten: 'If you are really a friend of Kurt Menke you will persuade him to go home. He has been foolish, but it is not too late for him to confess his errors.'

There was no signature and Charles gave an involuntary shiver as he read it a second time. Its quiet note of menace was enhanced by the thought that while he had been sitting inside the house someone had come up to his front-door and slid it stealthily through the letter box.

CHAPTER XVI

ALTHOUGH far from being a sybarite himself, Wragg considered that Brigstock carried austerity to an unwarrantable degree. The truth was, of course, that he just didn't notice his surroundings. No principles of asceticism were involved, it was just a case of unnoticed discomfort.

'Have some more coffee,' Brigstock said nodding at the ancient Thermos flask on his desk.

'No thanks.'

It had been cold and greasy half an hour ago and now would be even more disgusting.

'Sure? I'm going to.' He reached for the flask and poured the remains of the coffee into his cup. 'Quite sure?' he asked before putting it to his mouth.

'Certain.'

'Don't know what I'd do without a supply of coffee,' he remarked, licking his lips and replacing his pipe between his teeth. He looked at his watch. 'I doubt whether we're going to hear anything from Bowyer before the morning.'

'I didn't think we should. It's bound to take him a bit of time.'

'Strikes me as being very much a hit or miss sort of chap. I imagine his successes are coups of a really triumphant order and his failures are equally spectacular.'

'I'm afraid I always suspect his brand of virtuosity.'

'I know you do and you shouldn't make it so obvious.' A toothy grin accompanied the remark, to which Wragg responded with a severe frown. He knew he had his faults, but at least they weren't those of a prima donna.

Brigstock went on unconcernedly. 'What do you make of Menke's admission to Ashmore of having gone to the Old Bailey this afternoon and of actually being the person who flicked down the piece of paper?'

'I think it shows what a clever person we have on our hands. Never tell lies if you can avoid it. Admit as much as you can, but put your own gloss on events. Far fewer people would get caught out if they heeded that rule, whether they're murderers or adulterers. The only safe time to tell a lie is when you know it can never be proved against you.'

'Do you think Menke may have suspected he was being watched all the time?'

'I've thought about that. I'm sure he didn't suspect the whole thing was arranged; on the other hand it would be second nature to him to be as wary as a fox. So tell the truth about what you did and give it an innocent explanation.'

'Is he really that cunning?'

Wragg shot him a look of surprise. 'A K.G.B. man!'

'If he is! Anyway, not everyone in the K.G.B. is a genius, any more than everyone in our service has an I.Q. of a hundred and seventy. It's a matter of horses for courses.'

'If he's not a K.G.B. man, what is he?'

Brigstock sucked noisily on his pipe. 'I'm not saying he's not. I'm merely saying I'm not a hundred per cent satisfied he is.'

'That means doubting Bowyer's contact in Berlin.'

'Well?' Wragg looked nonplussed and Brigstock went on, 'I'd have thought you'd be among the last to have blind faith in one of Bowyer's stringers.'

'One has to hang on to something, otherwise it's like being on quicksands. My starting point is acceptance of the tip-off we got from Berlin.'

'It wasn't this morning when we had our meeting across the park,' Brigstock observed with a glint. 'You expressed yourself very much in favour of Bowyer going to Berlin so he could check personally that V hadn't been feeding us false information.

'That was this morning,' Wragg said testily. 'Menke's behaviour this afternoon has persuaded me he's a plant.'

'And the physical attack on him and Ashmore yesterday? How does that fit in?'

'I don't yet pretend to see how all the pieces fit together. After all, if you believe he's a plant then the assault business isn't consistent with such belief. And if you think he's a genuine defector, his behaviour this afternoon isn't consistent with that. So there are irreconcilables whatever you believe.'

Brigstock wiped a trickle of dribble from his chin and put his pipe lovingly back into his mouth.

'One thing for sure. If he is a plant, then Ragnold would seem to be connected in some way with his fake defection.'

'Correct. It must be so.' He glanced at the green phone on Brigstock's desk. 'Can I call the crytograph people to find out if they've had any luck with that piece of paper?'

'Go ahead. But they'd have let us know if they had.'

Wragg dialled a couple of digits and stood frowning at the floor while he waited for an answer.

'Alan? John Wragg here——Yes, that's what I was ringing about——Not yet——? When do you think——? O.K.,
but do your best, it's vital we know——' He replaced the
receiver and turned to Brigstock. 'Alan says it's either the
code for starting world war three or it's something out of a
packet of Rice Krispies.'

CHAPTER XVII

THE train pulled out of the Lehrter Station and had scarcely
gathered speed before it slowed down to pass over the wall
which stretched beneath its arches. Fierce white lights illu-
minated the killing ground which lay behind the wall and
comprised a broad strip of carefully tended sand, resem-
bling a never-used running track. Armed guards kept it
under a twenty-four hour surveillance and from time to
time inspected it for invisible footprints.

The train crawled on under the impassive gaze of a pair
of sentries standing beside the line. Bowyer stared out over
their heads at Berlin's famous Charité Hospital which lay
just within the border of the eastern sector. Its appearance
always reminded him of one of America's ivy league univer-
sities.

A minute or two later they came to a halt in Friedrichstrasse Station and Bowyer and his two dozen or so fellow
passengers got out. Most of them were Asian students bent
on a night out among the fleshpots of the Karl Marx Allee.
There were a few elderly Germans who had probably been
paying a prized and long-awaited visit to relations in West
Berlin and were now returning home. Their expressions
gave nothing away, but each of them was carrying a bag
which bulged with the outpouring of gifts they had received.
Gifts of those items which it was impossible to buy in the
capital of the D.D.R. as East Berlin proclaimed itself to the
arriving visitor.

Bowyer pushed his way past a throng of chattering Japanese and descended the staircase which led to the bleak room on the ground floor of the station which was used for immigration and customs inspections.

Though he didn't wish to give the impression of knowing the ropes too well, he equally didn't want to waste more time than was necessary in completing the formalities. And for all the welcoming notices and gay posters, no one could be more po-faced and bloody-minded than those whose job it was to ensure that no unwanted fish slipped through the meshes of their nets.

He filled in a form declaring the currency in his possession, handed it with his passport—or rather, with Sean O'Riordan's passport—to an unsmiling young Vopo and joined the band of others who were waiting to be admitted to the D.D.R. and who were sitting on hard benches with expressions which ranged from resignation to faint apprehension.

From time to time a loudspeaker crackled into life and reeled off a list of numbers in German. Those who were able to understand and to recognize their own reference being called out, trotted away to reclaim their passports and pass through another gloomy labyrinth of the station towards the street beyond.

On two occasions the young Vopo who handed out the forms and received them back remonstrated angrily in German with some unfortunate who had no idea what he'd done wrong or what he had to do right in order to get out of this oppressive limbo from which you could neither move forwards nor backwards until some unseen tyrant willed it.

Bowyer would have liked to have stepped forward and have helped these hapless offenders of bureaucratic red tape, but this was something Sean O'Riordan dared not do. One of them was a graceful Indian woman in a sari who retreated before the incomprehensible tirade and went and sat numbly in a corner of the room while tears slowly welled up in her eyes and began to trickle down her soft brown cheeks.

The party of Japanese students who had got off the same train as Bowyer arrived in the room ten minutes after him.

97

They merely burst into giggles when the Vopo indignantly tore up one of their forms which had been completed with a series of crosses.

Bowyer was glad to see that one of the Japanese girls went over to the Indian woman. As he well knew this whole unseemly charade was designed solely to obtain a signature from every entrant: a signature to ensure that those who later left were the self-same persons as those who had entered. That no one who entered could remain unaccounted for and that no one could leave unless the D.D.R. wished him to.

Bowyer heard his number called out and automatically glanced at his watch. He had been waiting just twenty-five minutes.

He passed through a door at the end of the room and joined a short queue. The queue moved forward and Bowyer came face to face with an unsmiling man who gave him a long hard look before examining his passport photograph and who then proceeded to compare the signature on his currency declaration form with that in the passport.

Jerome Bowyer watched him without a flicker of expression on his own face. It was not the moment for Sean O'Riordan to dance a jig.

The customs inspection which followed was perfunctory and then he passed through a grimy glass-panelled door out into the street. He hailed a taxi and told the driver to take him to the Budapest Restaurant on the Karl Marx Allee which was now the centre of East Berlin's entertainment world.

Unter den Linden and Friedrichstrasse which had once been the throbbing pulse of Berlin life were almost deserted at this dinner hour. The opera house was lit up and on the opposite side of the famous thoroughfare stood two motionless sentries outside the memorial erected to the victims of fascism and militarism. It was an apparently unnoticed irony that when the guard changed they goose-stepped with as much military precision as any of Hitler's soldiers.

The taxi rattled across the vast expanse of the Marx-Engels Platz where the regime now held its most important parades, past the base of the television tower, to emerge suddenly into the new East Berlin of modern buildings which resembled nothing so much as identical slabs lying in varying upturned positions.

He paid off the taxi and watched it drive away. Then he walked to the nearest U-Bahn Station and took a train to the end of the line. V lived about ten minutes' walk from there, in a flat with his widowed mother. It was a drab, working class district with few attractions.

As he stepped out of the underground station, he turned up the collar of his coat and walked with a purposeful air. Nobody would expect to see tourists here in the daytime, let alone after dark.

It was a cold night and there was a slight flurry of snow. The streets were deserted and the few people who were about showed no inclination to linger.

He turned into the street where V lived and slowed his pace as he peered intently towards one of the windows of the flat. But it was impossible to identify it with certainty from this distance. As he got closer he counted the floors from the bottom up and then the windows along on the fourth floor.

Yes, that was definitely their window and, moreover, it was dark. If anyone were at home there would almost certainly be a light showing. But the absence of light mightn't mean anything more than that V was out for the evening. And his mother, though old, quite often visited friends in the area, particularly when her son was not going to be in.

By now he had arrived outside the entrance to the block of flats. He had known all along what he would do, whether there was sign of life or not. He walked on and made his way back to the underground station where he found a public telephone. A few minutes later he was satisfied that there was, indeed, no one at home.

He would have made the call without first going near the flat, except for some innate sense of caution which invariably came into action when he was planning something, but which did nothing to prevent his subsequently taking calculated risks when executing his plan. He now hurried back to the street where V lived and entered the building. There was a decrepit lift which he ignored, choosing to ascend by the bare stone staircase. The whole interior had a seedy, run-down appearance. It was a block which had survived war-time bombing and been neglected ever since. Redecoration now would only emphasise its dowdiness. But to Jerome Bowyer it was unchanged from his last visit two years before.

He reached the fourth floor and pressed the bell of flat sixteen. As he had expected, there was no answer. On the opposite side of the landing stood the door of number eighteen. A light showed beneath it. He went across and rang the bell. The door was opened by a plump, middle-aged woman in a pinafore.

'I wonder if you can tell me when Frau Grisinger is expected home?' he said in German, 'My name is Pick. I'm in Berlin on business for a few days and some friends of Frau Grisinger's in Leipzig asked me to give her their greetings.'

'She went away suddenly a few days ago,' the woman said with a shrug. 'Her sister in Halle is sick.'

'Oh, I'm sorry to hear that. Does she not have a son living with her? My friends mentioned a son, I think——'

The woman looked suddenly flustered. 'Ja, ja,' she exclaimed, in an animated burst, 'but he is out, too. He will be back later. Give me your telephone number Herr Pick and I will tell him to call you. He would wish to talk to you.'

'I'm afraid the friends I'm staying with are not on the phone, but could you tell him I'll come back tomorrow evening at about this time?'

'Yes, he will be here, I know. I will tell him that you come. You mustn't disappoint him.'

'I certainly wouldn't do that. You've been most kind, Frau——'

'Koch.'

'Frau Koch. Please greet Herr Grisinger for me and tell him I look forward to seeing him tomorrow evening. Gute nacht.'

'Gute nacht, Herr Pick.'

Fifty minutes later, he was back in the flat in West Berlin. Getting out of the D.D.R.'s capital was always easier than getting in, provided, of course, you weren't one of its own subjects.

But for Jerome Bowyer, it had been fifty minutes of intensive thinking, for tomorrow, he had soon realized, was going to be another climactic day in his life.

CHAPTER XVIII

WRAGG drove down to 'Lakeside' early the next morning, intending to have breakfast when he arrived.

He had hardly entered the house before Hyde came hurrying out of the dining-room and, motioning Wragg to follow him, passed into the living-room on the other side of the hall.

'I take it our friend is having breakfast? Wragg said, after closing the door behind him.

'Yes. He's in a funny sort of mood this morning. Prickly and querulous.'

'He's been like that before.'

'Today he's more so.'

'After yesterday's performance, it's not surprising. He's putting up a front. Has he made any reference to yesterday?'

'Only to say we didn't look after him properly. Or rather that I didn't.'

'Well, I'll go and talk to him myself in a moment. I want some breakfast anyway.'

'He wants to see you.'

'Has he said so?'

'Yes. The first thing he said when he appeared this morning was what time would you be here?'

'Perhaps he's going to embellish the account he gave in Ashmore's office yesterday evening.'

'Any news from Berlin yet?'

'No. Not a word.'

'I suppose Bowyer's O.K.'

'What do you mean?' Wragg's tone was sharp.

'Nothing except that I'd never be surprised to learn he was working for the other side.'

'Do you have any reason for saying that?'

'No. It's just that he strikes me as being a rather mercurial type.'

'It's what he is, but that doesn't mean to say he's unreliable.'

Hyde shrugged. 'I thought you felt rather the same about him?'

'It's time I went and talked to Menke,' Wragg said firmly. Whatever his views of Bowyer, he didn't intend canvassing them with a relatively junior member of the service such as Hyde. The thing about Bowyer was that he did give such an impression. Moreover, he was aware of it and didn't care a damn. He had obviously been vetted with the thoroughness that all members of their two services underwent. But it was still a fact of life, of which no one was better aware than an interrogator such as Wragg, that living a lie could become an undetectable part of someone's existence. Most people were successful in concealing from those around them what they didn't wish to reveal. This certainly applied to those engaged in the profession of spying. Spies became unstuck through the defection of other spies, rarely through their own ineptitude. To them it was no more difficult to lead a double or treble life than it was to breathe.

Wragg crossed the hall and entered the dining-room. Kurt Menke was sitting staring gloomily out of the window with a cup of coffee clasped in his two hands.

'Ah!' he said with a note of triumph when he saw Wragg. 'Still the English cannot make coffee.'

'You can have tea if you'd prefer it.'

'Tea for breakfast! It is better to have a cup of water.'

Wragg buttered a piece of toast and poured himself some coffee. 'I want to talk to you.'

'And *I* want to talk to you.'

'Go ahead.'

Kurt put down his cup and fixed Wragg with a grave look. 'I do not sleep last night because I have been thinking. My mind has been working all the time. You can tell, hein?' He pointed at his eyes which were red and lustreless and gingerly touched the bags beneath them, as though they might at any moment descend his cheeks like avalanches. 'I wish to go home,' he said after a dramatic pause.

'Back to Germany, you mean?' Wragg enquired mildly.

'Of course Germany. Germany is my home.'

Wragg peered out of the window as though considering a request from a small boy to go and play in the garden.

'Why have you suddenly decided you want to go back?' he asked in the same mildly interested tone.

'I realize I have made a big mistake. I was foolish. I acted on a compulse.'

'Impulse.'

'Yes, on an impulse. London went to my head and I suddenly think I must stay here for ever. I will phone my old friend, Charles Ashmore, and he will be able to help me stay.' His tone became accusing. 'I do not expect to be held like this and asked all these questions. You have not treated me like a guest. I do not think you really want me. You are only interested in what I can tell you about my own country. You make me feel like I am a traitor.' He paused again and added dramatically, 'And that, my friend, I do not like! I am not a traitor. I am a free individual except that you do not let me be one. If I go back now, I may be punished, I realize that, but it is better than to be a lonely exile in an unfriendly country. The English are not simpatico to strangers, is it not always said so? I have found it for myself It is not your fault, it is your natures. So it is better that I go home, have my punishment and live again among my own people. You are surprised by what I say, hein? But it is never too late to repair!'

Wragg who had listened impassively slowly lit a cigarette.

'This is just a normal reaction to recent events,' he remarked in a matter-of-fact voice. 'In twenty-four hours' time you'll be begging to stay again.'

Kurt's face suffused with anger.

'You treat me like a child. You do not believe what I tell you, but I am in earnest. I have been thinking all night and I want to go back. I am definite, so there is no more to be said.'

'You're obviously somebody who undergoes changes of mind. Well, there's nothing wrong about that provided you recognize the fact and don't act like a weathercock on a gusty day.'

Kurt frowned furiously. 'I do not understand. What is a weathercock? And a gusty day? What is gusty?'

'Weathercocks are those things you see on tops of churches which show which way the wind is blowing. Sometimes they spin wildly this way and that when the wind is coming in gusts from different directions.

'And I am like that?' His tone was explosive.

'Yes.'

'It is not enough that you treat me like a criminal, that my life is threatened—yes, threatened, my friend! Was I being a weathercock when I was attacked on your peaceful Sussex hills?'

Wragg shrugged. 'If they did that to you in England, how much worse is it going to be when they get you back?'

'I tell you, I am ready for punishment.' His tone became martyred.

'But what punishment?'

'Some months in prison?'

'Is that all?'

'They will be merciful if I show real repentance.'

'If you return now, the odds are you'll forfeit your life.'

'It is not true——'

'You will disappear as completely as if you'd fallen down a disused mine shaft. The K.G.B. will liquidate you before you've been back ten minutes.'

Kurt had gone suddenly tense. 'K.G.B.! That is a Russian organization. We do not have a K.G.B. in Germany. Why do you say the K.G.B. to me?'

'You know as well as I do that the K.G.B. have links in East Germany.'

'But why should they be interested in me?'

'They're interested in everyone who defects from the Soviet empire. You know it was the K.G.B. who attacked you and Ashmore up on the Downs last Sunday, don't you?'

'That is why I am frightened. That is why I want to go home before it is too late.'

'It's already too late.'

'No, no, it is not. I want to go now. Today.'

'It couldn't possibly be arranged before tomorrow.'

'You mean, I may go home tomorrow?' he said eagerly.

'Oh, it doesn't rest with me. It's a matter for my superiors.'

'But you will tell them?'

'I'll certainly tell them, but I don't know what their reaction will be.'

'You must plead for me, yes?'

'All I can do is pass on your request for repatriation, but I'm afraid they'll be puzzled. This abrupt change of heart, I mean. It'll make them suspicious.'

'But you believe me?'

'I think perhaps I do,' he said slowly.

Kurt let out a sigh. 'If you believe me, I am sure you will make the others, too.'

'It doesn't follow.'

'If I can leave tomorrow——'

'Don't depend on it. These return trips can't be fixed up like a day at the seaside. Particularly as your country has no diplomatic representative here, only a trade mission.'

'Yes, but they would help with the arrangements.'

'I don't think my people would approve of that. You'll probably just have to be slipped through the wall at one of the crossing-points.'

Kurt nodded obediently. 'I will trust you, because I now know you understand.'

'If I help you, then you've got to help me,' Wragg said in a brisk change of tone.

'I do not know how I can help you.'

'I'll tell you. It's quite simple: just tell me the truth. Why did you defect?'

'But I have told.'

'Sure, but this time the truth.'

'I thought you believe me,' Kurt said in a huffed voice. 'Now I think you just play with me.'

'You started the game.'

'I do not understand.'

'You've been playing with us ever since you telephoned Ashmore that evening last week. However, let me help. What's your interest in Ragnold?'

'He is Charles Ashmore's customer.'

'I know he's his client, but why are you interested in him?'

'I have no interest in that man. I do not know anything about him.'

'I don't believe that.'

Kurt gave a gigantic shrug as though to heave off the burden of accusations which were being thrust on him.

'But I tell you I don't know him.'

'You mayn't know him, but you're interested in him.

'No, no.'

'That piece of paper you flicked down from the public gallery yesterday afternoon, it was a message for Ragnold, wasn't it?'

'A message!' Kurt sounded incredulous.

'It was in code.'

'I throw the paper to try and catch Charles' attention.'

'You could have done that by sending him a message into Court.'

'Hein?'

'You understood!'

'But I explain yesterday at Charles' office.'

'You gave an explanation, but it wasn't the truth. If you were as frightened as you say you were, when you were left alone in the restaurant, why did you go out into the street and take a taxi to the Old Bailey?'

'To find Charles. He is my only friend in London. It is natural that I turn to him.'

'You realize that, when we've decoded the message, your lies will be shown up.'

'You are mad, mad! I do not know why you say these things.'

'Well, if you want me to help you, you'd better think about it. I want the truth about your interest in Ragnold before I start helping you.'

While Wragg had been speaking, Kurt's expression had become closed in like a fogbound airport. Wragg observed this with satisfaction. The moment had come to leave him to sort out his thoughts. It had been a relief to be able to speak out in this particular confrontation and show the bastard a few of the cards in your hand. Not too many, mind you, but enough to give him food for thought.

Later when he reported on the interview to Brigstock, that worthy had said through a blanket of pipe smoke:

'Now, we'll see what he gets up to next. One thing for sure, he won't sit back and do nothing.'

'Exactly!'

CHAPTER XIX

So far as travelling between Brixton Prison and the Old Bailey was concerned, Ragnold was accorded V.I.P. treatment. Instead of being incarcerated in one of the tiny cells of the prison van which threaded its way at a sedate pace through the morning and evening traffic of South London, he made the journey in a private car seated in the back beside a Detective Sergeant of the Special Branch.

The car was an ordinary saloon which mingled anonymously with several hundred others of similar appearance, all heading towards the centre of town in the morning rush hour.

The only distinction between it and the others lay with its back seat passengers, who were hand-cuffed together. But unobtrusively so that no one happening to look in would notice anything untoward.

His escort had long since given up trying to make conversation on the trip as the prisoner had made it clear that he preferred to sit in silence with his own thoughts.

During the earlier days of the trial, before his escort had exhausted his conversational gambits, Ragnold had appeared to listen attentively to anything said to him, though he had never responded with more than an agreeable smile or a small nod, and just occasionally the briefest of verbal comment.

The reason for what appeared to be a thoroughly enigmatic silence was simpler than anyone guessed. It was just that he enjoyed the twice daily ride through London's busy streets and didn't wish to miss anything in the passing scene. Conversation in the circumstances was a distraction to be avoided.

He was a man of considerable fortitude and he had had time to prepare himself for the long period ahead when he would be seeing none of the sights which now greeted his eyes. Women with prams, old men sitting on seats, dogs sniffing at lamp posts and shop windows stuffed with enticing bargains on easy credit terms.

He felt reasonably certain he would be convicted and, if convicted, he knew he would receive a very long sentence. He felt wholly unemotional at the prospect and was able to view it without a vestige of self-pity.

He had played the game according to established rules and looked like losing. British justice seemed about to snatch its victim, British feelings of outrage and affront had to be assuaged. The judge would deliver a homily about treachery and disgrace which would leave him unmoved.

It secretly amused him to keep everyone puzzled as to his motives and the extent of the so-called treachery. Not that he assumed his attitude merely to be self-indulgent. The only person he felt a bit sorry for was Charles Ashmore with his perpetually worried air. In different circumstances he would have rather enjoyed his company. As it was, it was painfully obvious that his efforts to make his solicitor more at ease were singularly unsuccessful. He supposed this was inevitable, given the context of their relationship.

As the car passed through the main gates of Brixton Prison on its journey to the Old Bailey that Tuesday morning, he hummed softly beneath his breath. Today it cut across the main road and dived among the vestiges of terraced Victorian villas which had survived the greedy clutches of the developers.

The route varied from day to day, which, so far as Ragnold was concerned, added to the interest.

'You're humming again,' the Special Branch officer at his side said in an accusing tone.

'I'm sorry. I forgot it irritated you.'

'I wouldn't mind if you sang a few choruses at the top of your voice. It's that humming under your breath that gets on one's nerves.'

'I'll try to remember.'

'Here, have a cigarette. You can't smoke and hum at the same time.'

'Thanks.'

'Give us a light, Tom,' he said to the officer sitting beside the driver. 'You know I can't manage on my own with us like a pair of bloody Siamese twins.'

The one called Tom turned, it seemed reluctantly, and lit first Ragnold's cigarette and then his escort's. When he turned back, he glanced in the rear-view mirror and frowned.

'That Cortina's been behind us for the past ten minutes,' he said to the driver in a wary tone.

The driver's eyes flicked up to the mirror. 'I know, I've been watching him. I think he's probably harmless. He's all alone and he looks a pretty skinny type.'

'Let's make sure. Slow down and wave him past.'

'Right.'

As events turned out, there was no need for the Cortina suddenly indicated a right turn and disappeared from view up a road behind them.

'So much for him,' the driver said nonchalantly.

Ragnold, who had been listening to all this with a small smile, began to hum again.

'Oh, no, I can't take it!' his escort exclaimed with exasperation.

'Was I doing it again?'

'Yes, you bloody well were.'

'I'm sorry.'

'Wouldn't you like to talk for a change?'

'What about?'

'You name it, I'll try and keep up.'

'I don't think I particularly want to talk. I just enjoy looking out of the car window.'

'If you don't mind my saying so, you're an extraordinary chap.'

'Oh?'

'Most people enjoy talking after being shut up in Brixton all night. It makes them feel normal again.'

Ragnold turned his head to give his escort a bland smile. 'If you don't mind *my* saying so, it's obviously not only those who spend their nights at Brixton who have an urge to talk.'

Tom in the front seat gave a snigger while the escort vented the loud sigh of an ill-used victim.

'All right, don't talk,' he said sourly, 'but for God's sake, don't hum either.'

It was about twenty minutes later than Tom said in an irritable tone, 'Why the hell did you choose Blackfriars Bridge? It's always impossible at this hour.'

'They all are,' the driver said placidly. 'Anyway, it was Blackfriar's turn.'

'It wasn't bad yesterday using Waterloo bridge.'

The driver sighed. 'Take a different route each day, those are the orders. And at some points we have to cross old Father Thames . . .'

'Bloody river and its bloody congested bridges!'

'Relax. Enjoy the scenery like our guest in the back.'

'I've got this feeling in my water something's going to go wrong today.'

The driver laughed. 'Your water's about as reliable as a weather forecast. Anyway, we're almost there. You can see the Old Bailey. Look . . .'

'You don't need to tell me which the Old Bailey is! But at this rate of progress it'll still take us another fifteen minutes.'

'It won't, you know. The traffic's started to move ahead. We'll be there in three minutes. And a good job, too, with you as jumpy as you are.'

'It's all right for you, you're only the driver. I'm the one who carries the can if anything goes wrong.'

The driver sighed again. Tom had these sort of days and there was nothing you could do save put up with him as best you could. He'd been a bag of nerves since the time he'd gone over to Belfast on a special assignment and been caught in a bomb explosion. The man next to him had caught the full force and, apart from a shoe with a foot in it, nothing of him had ever been found. Such are the vagaries

110

of blast that Tom who had been only six feet away suffered nothing worse than three months of deafness—and shock.

He had only been back on full duty a few weeks and though he was fine for most of the time, there were days such as these when his raw nerve ends showed through, which was, the driver supposed, understandable in the circumstances.

Ragnold had appeared undisturbed by the front-seat altercation. Indeed, the longer the journey lasted, the more he enjoyed it. He had, however, begun to hum quietly under his breath again. His escort had thrown him a look of disgust, which he hadn't intercepted, but had obviously now concluded that this was something which also had to be put up with, like Tom's jumpiness.

The car was now only eighty yards from its destination and the driver was getting ready to swing into the prisoners' entrance.

Suddenly from the left a grey van backed slowly, but inexorably across their path.

'Christ! Watch out for that stupid bugger!' Tom shouted.

At the same time, the driver flashed his headlights and pressed on the horn.

But still the van came slowly on.

'Drive up on the pavement,' Tom yelled, 'you've got to get past.'

The car bucked as the off-side front wheel struck the kerb. There was a loud bang as the tyre burst and the rear of the car came round in a vicious arc to catch the van amidships.

The familiar sounds of tearing metal and shattering glass gave way to the equally familiar, and almost more sinister, silence which settles for a second or two after an accident. Then there was shouting and the sounds of people running.

Ragnold's escort looked at his charge. At least he was still in the car. He'd half-expected to find an empty handcuff dangling from his wrist and was relieved to know that whatever had happened and whatever the intention had been, the prisoner was safe.

'That's stopped his humming,' he thought to himself as he put a hand up to Ragnold's lolling head.

Which was true, for Evelyn Ragnold was dead.

111

CHAPTER XX

WHEN Charles Ashmore arrived at Court about forty minutes after the accident, he noticed that the nearby street was
cordoned off and that the area was swarming with police.
However, he was already a few minutes late and he hurried
inside the building without pausing to satisfy his curiosity
as to what had happened.

He was on his way up the main staircase when he heard
his name being called and turned to find Martin Ainsworth's
clerk chasing after him.

'You've heard the news, Mr. Ashmore?' Donald enquired
breathlessly.

'I've heard nothing. I've only just arrived.'

'The car bringing Major Ragnold from Brixton was
involved in an accident and he's been killed.'

Charles took a pace back and leant against the marble
balustrade. His immediate reaction was one in which relief
was uppermost. Not relief for himself, but for his old
friend, Evelyn Ragnold's father, who would now be spared
the additional shame which conviction and sentence couldn't
have failed to bring.

'Is that what that crowd down the street is about?'

'Yes. It seems a van backed out into the path of the car
and the driver couldn't avoid the accident.'

'What about the other people in the car?'

'Shaken up, but not badly injured.'

'And the van driver?'

'He scarpered in the confusion which followed. No one
seems to have seen him.'

Charles frowned. Pray God this was a straightforward
death as a result of an ordinary accident. The fact that the
driver of the other vehicle had run off afterwards didn't
destroy that hope, but it certainly didn't enchance it either.

'Here's Mr. Ainsworth now,' Donald said, 'he'll be able to
tell you more, sir.'

'You've heard what's happened?' Martin Ainsworth said
with a grim expression.

'I've heard that Ragnold lost his life in this car accident.'

'Come up to Court and I'll tell you all I know. I've just been talking to the police, though they're still in the position of trying to fit the pieces together. Meanwhile, the rumours are as wild as any you could think up.'

Charles picked up his briefcase which he had put on the stair beside him and followed his leading Counsel up to Court Number One.

Ainsworth peered through an outer glass door and shuddered. 'It looks like the floor of the Stock Exchange after a market crash. We'll go and find a quiet corner in the judges' corridor. I'm due to sit here as a recorder next month so it'll only be anticipating events,' he added with a wry smile.

They passed through a set of swing doors into the cloistral calm of the judges' quarters. A thick carpet seemed to absorb such sounds as anyone could make and the atmosphere was as different from that on the farther side of the doors as the headmaster's study from the junior dormitory.

'Let's perch here,' Ainsworth said seating himself on a window ledge. 'Cigarette?' He inhaled deeply. 'They'll be running round in circles for a while yet. The only thing for certain is that Ragnold is dead. What he died of nobody knows. It could have been as a result of the accident: it could have been something more sinister.' Charles glanced at him sharply. 'Yes, they're even ready to believe he may have been murdered. Poison needle or something of that sort.'

'Is there any evidence to support such an improbable theory?' Charles asked in an incredulous tone.

'It seems that somebody opened the passenger door on Ragnold's side as soon as the car came to rest.'

'Probably a rescuer.'

'I agree. It might well have been, but, as I say, they're ready to believe anything at the moment. No possibility, however fantastic, is being excluded. Also, if it was a rescuer, he didn't hang around afterwards. Like the driver of the van, he melted away.'

'That doesn't particularly surprise me. Most people try and avoid becoming involved as witnesses in traffic accidents.'

'I agree, though it's a bit different with the driver.'

'He must have panicked.'

'That's obviously a possibility. Anyway, they should be able to trace the van without much difficulty and, provided it's all above board, that'll lead them to the driver.'

'And if it's not all above board?'

'A whole range of further possibilities will be opened up, won't they?' He studied the tip of his cigarette. 'I think we have to accept that our client had become cloaked with an unusual amount of mystery. Unusual, that is, even in an Official Secrets Act case. He's had the authorities groping in the dark from the outset. I don't doubt that they know a bit more than has emerged in public. They always do. But it's obvious they've not found out as much as they would like. Ragnold hadn't proved very co-operative.'

'You mean he hadn't confessed?'

'Confessions and co-operation are synonymous in this context.'

'But who wanted to murder him?'

Ainsworth shrugged. 'If we knew that, we'd know a great deal. The life of a spy must hang on a brittle thread at all times. I've had some personal experience of the world in which they move, and I can only say that it's like picking your way across a terrain of lurking menace. It looks innocent enough to the casual glance, but there's the equivalent of a black widow spider in every shadowy corner.'

Charles had heard that Martin Ainsworth had been concerned in one or two exploits for the secret service, though he was unaware of the details.

'Anyway,' Ainsworth went on, 'it looks like the end of the case as far as we're concerned. Whatever our client died of is irrelevant to the termination of his trial, though I imagine you will be left with rather more pieces to sweep up than I shall.'

'I imagine so. Solicitors normally are!'

Ainsworth smiled. 'That's why I went to the criminal Bar. Very little sweeping up there.' He looked at his watch. 'We'd better get along to Court for the final formalities.'

'What exactly is going to happen?'

'The judge will already have been told, of course. However, he'll have to be told officially in open Court. He'll probably hear formal evidence of Ragnold's death just for the Court record and then he'll discharge the jury. And that'll be the end of that.'

'And the beginning of a lot of other things,' Charles murmured, more to himself than to Ainsworth who had already moved off down the corridor.

CHAPTER XXI

SITTING in the taxi on his way back to his office, Charles Ashmore tried to persuade himself that what had happened had happened for the best, however, callous this sounded. Even for Evelyn Ragnold himself, he found it possible to think that death had released him from a grim and hopeless—yes, hopeless—future.

The first thing he must do when he got back was put through a phone call to Ragnold Hall and break the news to the old man. It wasn't a task he relished, but he hoped he'd be ahead of a newscast. Even now the news must be humming over the wires and through the ether. A newsvendor's placard caught his eye.

'Spy Trial Sensation.'

His secretary, Miss Acres, rushed out of her room as he entered the main door. This in itself was an omen, as she was normally the most equable and unflappable of women.

'Sir Wilfred has just been on the phone from Lincolnshire,' she said breathlessly. 'He'd apparently heard a news flash that Major Ragnold was dead. I told him that you would call him back as soon as you could.'

'When did you hear the news?'

'I didn't. That's what made it so awful.' Her tone became reproachful. 'I went straightaway and spoke to Mr. Quigley and he didn't know anything either, but he telephoned the Old Bailey and was told that it was true.'

115

'I'm sorry,' Charles said with a note of weary penitence, 'but I thought I'd be back before the news broke. I clearly misjudged the speed with which these things get disseminated. You'd better get Sir Wilfred for me right away.'

Miss Acres scurried back into her own small domain and Charles entered his rather grander adjoining room. He had scarcely taken off his hat and coat when the phone on his desk gave a discreet tinkle and he went across and picked up the receiver.

'I have Sir Wilfred Ragnold on the line, Mr. Ashmore,' Miss Acres said in her most secretaryish voice.

'Hello, Wilfred, I'm dreadfully sorry that I was unable to get you before you heard the news about Evelyn over the radio.'

'That's all right. Difficult to be ahead of these reporter blighters nowadays. I've already had three calls from newspapers.'

'Oh, no!'

'Don't worry. I'm not speaking to any of them and I've told Mrs. Marks to put down the receiver as soon as they've established themselves as newspaper people. At least, Charles, you'll be able to tell me exactly what happened.' The old man's voice sounded robust, despite the appalling shock he must have received.

'There was a car crash only a few yards from the Old Bailey. The car bringing Evelyn to Court collided with a van and Evelyn was killed.'

'That's what they said on the radio.'

'That's all we know at the moment. When I left the Old Bailey about twenty minutes ago, nothing further had emerged.'

'Evelyn was the only one to lose his life?'

'Yes. Of course, there'll be a post mortem and meanwhile the police are investigating the details of the accident.'

'I follow.'

'The best thing will be, Wilfred, if I call you back this afternoon. Or earlier if I hear anything. What about Evelyn's wife?'

'I'll speak to her myself.'

'And advise her not to talk to the press for the time being.'

'I shall do more than advise her!' There was a pause, then the old man said in a curiously wistful voice, 'Sometimes it's best to know the worst.' The tone changed abruptly as he almost immediately went on, 'I'll await your further call, Charles. Good-bye.'

As Charles replaced the receiver, his senior partner sidled into the room. Charles gave him what he hoped was a reasonably dispassionate welcome. Not that Walter Quigley had ever been sensitive to atmosphere, as his opening remark confirmed.

'Well! I suppose that's about the best thing that could have happened. Best from everyone's point of view, the tax payers, his family's and, not least, Quigley, Smith's. It was a genuine accident, I imagine?'

'I've not heard to the contrary,' Charles replied.

'Incidentally, I've told the new girl on the switchboard to block all calls from the press. You don't want to speak to them, do you?'

'No, but is that fair on her? They can be very persistent.'

'Have them put through to you if you want. I don't mind. Incidentally what's her name?'

'Whose?'

'The new switchboard girl.'

'Miss Speke, if you want to be formal. Otherwise Linda. And she's been here nearly three months.'

'So what?'

'You keep calling her new.'

Walter Quigley appeared to consider the criticism and dismiss it.

'I suppose Miss Acres told you that Wilfred Ragnold had been on the phone?

'Yes. I was speaking to him just before you came in.'

'How's he taken the news?'

'He sounded quite robust.'

'Must have come as a shock to him, but I imagine he'll see it as a relief. Terrible to have your only son turn traitor to his country.'

'He hadn't yet been convicted.'

Walter Quigley gave Charles a pitying look. 'Don't tell me you didn't perfectly well know what the jury's verdict was going to be.'

'It's exactly what I do tell you. It's the unpredictability of English juries that leaves a defendant's hope unquenched.'

'A defendant's maybe! But his legal adviser should have a better sense of the realities. Anyway, it's all academic and I still think it's the best thing that could have happened. What's more, I'm sure you do, too!'

There was a knock on the door and Miss Acres appeared.

'I apologise for interrupting you, but Mr. Wragg is here and wants to see you most urgently, Mr. Ashmore.'

'All right, I'll see him in a moment.'

'Client?' Walter Quigley enquired with curiosity.

'No, a member of the security service.'

Quigley permitted himself a mild, well-bred sneer. 'Well, I'd better leave you to your secret conclave with the gentleman. Incidentally, Celia asked me to give you some message or other, but I can't remember what it was.' He turned and strolled out of the room as it might be part of his own suite.

A minute later, Miss Acres opened the door to admit Wragg. As he came into the room, he dropped his raincoat on to a chair and carefully placed his hat on top of it. It was a cardboard-looking hat rather like the ones the army handed out to demobbed soldiers after the war. Charles had noticed that he was never without it.

'Thank you for seeing me at such short notice,' he said in his strangely neutral voice as he sat down in the chair which Charles motioned him towards. 'It's about Menke.'

'What this time?'

'Has he tried to get in touch with you since he turned up at your office yesterday afternoon?'

'No. He hasn't had much opportunity.'

Wragg shifted stiffly and gave Charles a long, hard look with eyes which put him in mind of a grey, winter sky.

'Can you think of anything at all in the Ragnold case which might have been of interest to Menke?' he asked in a tone which matched his expression.

'If Menke's interests are no more than he has declared them to be, the answer is no.'

'What do you mean by "declared them to be"?'

'As I've mentioned to you, he did tell me on that fateful Sunday we went up to Chanctonbury Ring that he had some sort of security job in a ministry. But it didn't sound very high-powered, even though he was the delegation's watchdog over here.'

'There's reason for believing that he's a rather more important cog than he's made out.'

'If he is, I don't know anything about it.'

'And that his defection isn't genuine.'

'I'd already gathered that. From you, that is.'

'There's also reason for believing,' Wragg went on as though Charles hadn't spoken, 'that his so-called defection is in some way connected with the Ragnold case.'

'If that's so, I'm afraid I can't help you.'

'You had no warning of Menke's arrival?'

'Absolutely none, until the evening he phoned me and I went out and picked him up at the Piccadilly Hotel.'

'He hadn't been in touch with you in the preceding weeks?'

'No. Anyway, isn't it too much of a coincidence that of all the solicitors in England who might have defended Evelyn Ragnold, it turns out to be one who had known Kurt all these years?'

'It needn't have been a coincidence at all. Look at it this way. The K.G.B. have this interest in the trial, whatever it is, and by good fortune they have someone to hand who is an old friend of someone intimately connected with the case. He becomes a natural choice for the assignment.'

'I see!'

'No coincidence at all.'

'But what about the assaults on us both at Chanctonbury Ring, they were genuine enough. How do they fit in with your theory that Kurt is a plant?'

'They can be seen as part of a plan to persuade us that he *is* a genuine defector whose life is in danger, as he alleges. It's just backing for his story.'

'Would they really go to those lengths?'

Wragg looked at him in genuine surprise. 'They'd go to a great many further lengths as well.' He gave Charles one of

119

his rare, if fleeting, smiles. 'And so would we! Believe me, Mr. Ashmore, nothing is too much trouble or too difficult or too costly when it comes to frustrating the other side.'

'So Kurt is a member of the K.G.B. who has come to this country under false colours for the purpose of doing something in connection with the Ragnold case? Is that it?'

'It's a theory.'

'But you don't know the specific matter which has brought him?'

'Correct. And that's why I'm here now and why I've taken you into my confidence.'

'But unfortunately I'm unable to help you. Evelyn Ragnold was as uncommunicative to me as he was to your people who interrogated him. If you think he confided snippets of secret information in me, you're absolutely wrong. He said nothing about the offence with which he was charged other than to deny it. Even if I was prepared to breach a client's confidence, there's nothing I could tell you.'

'Now he's a dead client.'

'Dead or alive, the facts are the same.' Charles paused and frowned slightly. 'You don't suggest that Kurt had anything to do with this morning's events outside the Old Bailey?'

'I neither suggest it nor do I dismiss the possibility. Particularly after Menke's strange behaviour yesterday when he slipped his lead and streaked off to the Old Bailey.'

'When are we likely to learn the result of the post mortem on my late client?'

'It may be a day or so before we get the final result. Various organs have got to be analysed and that takes time.'

'But surely there'll be some indication as to cause of death before then?'

'Possibly.'

'But you're not going to be satisfied until you have the result signed and sealed?'

'Correct.'

'Where is Kurt at the moment? Down at your country retreat?'

'Yes. I was there when I got the news of Ragnold's death.'

'Did you tell Kurt?'

'No. I've also made sure he doesn't find out until I want him to.' Wragg's eyes flicked at the wall he was facing like an adder's tongue. 'You were speaking of coincidences just now. Here's another one for you if you're minded to see it as such. At about the same moment as Ragnold was meeting his death, Menke was demanding that he be repatriated. Mission completed, as one might say!'

'What reason did he give you for wanting to go back?' Charles asked with a sudden quickening interest.

'Homesick. Made a big mistake. Unfriendly reception here. That was the general line.'

Charles felt inside his wallet pocket and pulled out an envelope.

'This was shoved through my letter-box sometime yesterday evening.'

Wragg read the note, turned it over, held it up to the light and finally put it down on Charles' desk.

'What have you done about it?'

'Until this moment of showing it to you, nothing.'

Wragg was thoughtful for over a minute. When he looked up, he said, 'Are you doing anything this evening?'

'Why?' Charles' tone was wary.

'Would you have Menke to dinner at your home in London?'

'Go on!'

'Show him that note and see how he reacts. If he tries to enlist your help in arranging his return home, play along with the idea. Be sympathetic and see what you can wheedle out of him. Talk to him freely. You can even express hostility towards my lot if you think it'll help to gain his confidence.'

Charles refrained from pointing out that that might come more easily than Wragg would prefer to know. Instead he said, 'What excuse will you give for bringing him to my place?'

'I'll say you extended the invitation. And you can make this note the reason for wanting to have a talk with him.'

'All right. I'll have him to dinner.'

'Seven-thirty?'

'Make it eight o'clock.'

121

CHAPTER XXII

BEFORE he left the office, Charles telephoned Sir Wilfred Ragnold to say that the result of the autopsy wouldn't be known for a day or two.

'He died as a result of a car accident, so what's the difficulty?' the old man commented, before adding, 'Not that it makes any odds.'

Charles had been disinclined to arouse what might be groundless anxieties as to what exactly had happened and was glad to murmur non-committally in reply. He gathered that the press had scarcely been off the line, but had been unable to penetrate the wall of silence behind which the family sat out the telephonic siege. Evelyn's wife and the children had now moved into Ragnold Hall.

After saying that he would come up to Lincolnshire as soon as things had sorted themselves out, he had rung off.

As he sat in a taxi on his way home that evening, he reached one of those sudden personal decisions, not particularly momentous in themselves, but which can act like a shot in the arm to a dying man. He would take a month's holiday at the earliest possible moment and get right away. No sooner was the decision made than he began to feel in better spirits and he spent the remainder of the journey contemplating the rival attractions of a sun-drenched beach and the clear, sparkling air of a mountain resort.

In the same mood, he poured himself a large whisky when he got in and took it up to his bedroom. After he had had a shower and changed, he came down and poured out another. Then he switched on the television and further relaxed in half an hour's mindless watching.

On the dot of eight o'clock a car drew up outside and a few seconds later he heard the front-door bell ring. The murmur of voices in the hall reached his ears and he got up to turn off the television. His period of relaxation was over, he reflected grimly as he waited for Kurt to be shown in. He wasn't particularly looking forward to the evening ahead.

'Ah, Charles, it is good that I see you again. I think

earlier I may not do so.' Kurt pumped his hand warmly by way of greeting. 'I have much to tell you and I am very happy when they say you have invited me to dinner at your home.'

'Let me get you a drink before we start talking, Kurt.'

'I will take some gin.'

'With anything?'

'No——but just a splash of water perhaps.'

Kurt sniffed at the glass which Charles handed him and then gulped down about half the contents.

'The drinks at that farm are for little girls.' he remarked, 'but this is a real drink.'

'You might as well let me re-fill your glass before we sit down,' Charles said.

'And now we can talk, yes?' Kurt sat back in a corner of the sofa sending out palpable waves of nervous combustibility, 'Charles, I must tell you at once, I am going home. It is nothing to do with you and I hope you will still be my friend. But I have made a terrible mistake and the sooner I go, the better it will be for me. Perhaps I expect too much here——' His tone hardened as he went on, 'But I do not expect what I get! I am treated like a criminal——my feelings are not realized. It is worse than the police in the D.D.R.——Anyway, I have decided.'

'Read this,' Charles said handing him the note which had been put through his letter-box the previous evening.

Kurt read it with frowning concentration.

'So!' His tone was thoughtful.

'Who do you imagine sent it to me?'

'I do not know, Charles, but it is someone who knows you are my friend.'

'From what you've just told me, I don't have to use my powers of persuasion. You've decided to go, anyway.'

'But this letter confirms that I make a right decision. You will show it to Wragg, yes?'

Charles side-stepped the question and said, 'Has Wragg agreed that you can go back?'

'Agreed?' Kurt's voice rose to an indignant squeak. 'He cannot stop me. I have not broken the law, I am a free person. I tell him I wish to go and I go.'

'But you will need his co-operation, surely, in the making of the arrangements?'

'Pah! You can make the so-called arrangements very quickly. I tell you, Charles,' he went on solemnly, 'that if I am still in England tomorrow night, I shall ask you to create a very big fuss with the government. This Wragg he tries to threaten me. But I am not to be threatened.'

'I confess that I'm not very taken with him myself.'

'He is like all secret police. They are not nice.'

It was at this moment Burden announced that dinner was ready. As though to speed Kurt on his way, Mrs. Burden had chosen this of all evenings to prepare a Hungarian Goulash, which they washed down with a bottle of claret. When they returned upstairs after the meal, Kurt once more took possession of the end of the sofa and Charles brought him a very large brandy and a cigar.

'What do you think will happen to you when you return?' he asked as he sat down.

'I shall be questioned. And if I admit my fault, they will be mild to me. I must expect some punishment, but it is better than to stay where I cannot be happy.'

'You must let me know how you get on.'

'Charles, we are always friends, yes? I cannot write to you at once as there may be difficulties, you understand. But I think of you and one day we communicate again.'

'Yes, of course.'

'But I do not send even a postcard to Wragg!'

Charles laughed. 'His trouble is that he suspects you of having deep, hidden motives. I told him originally I was sure you were a genuine defector, but I confess that I have wondered once or twice. Not that it makes any difference to me, we're old friends and you've now decided to go home. What's happened this past week is so much water under the bridge. But what is the truth?'

Kurt leant forward and, with an earnest, confidential air said, 'I do not deceive my friends, Charles. I do not deceive you.'

Even as he spoke, Charles realized that he hadn't really expected any other response. If Kurt was what Wragg believed him to be, it was hardly likely that he would immediately peel off his mask and reveal himself as a self-confessed secret agent at the first tug on the ties of a long if tenuous friendship. And yet it irked him that Kurt should now be gazing into his face with an expression of sincere appeal.

'Oh, come off it,' he said in a still amiable tone. 'You've behaved pretty oddly for a genuine defector——'

'You are saying I am a liar, Charles?' Kurt broke in indignantly.

'I don't know what I think.' Charles' tone was suddenly weary. 'Too much has happened too quickly and I haven't had time to catch my breath. But it doesn't matter—— you're about to go back——and it's anyway not my business.'

'But it is your business. I cannot leave unless you believe me. You have been good and kind to me.' He threw his arms out wide as if to expose his innocent breast to whatever further poisoned darts Charles was waiting to fire.

'Ask me questions, Charles. Any question you like and I will give you truthful answers.'

'Are you a member of the Russian K.G.B.?' Charles enquired somewhat in the tone of one embarking none too enthusiastically on a boring parlour game.

'It is rubbish.'

'Do you have a special interest in my late client, Evelyn Ragnold?'

'I have never met that man.'

Charles made a small gesture of distaste. He was suddenly feeling very tired and the situation had become ridiculous, even preposterous.

'Another question, Charles,' Kurt said dramatically.

'Let's stop this nonsense. Let's talk about something else. I'm sorry I started it.'

'You are upset, Charles?'

'I'm just tired.'

'Your daughter, she is not coming tonight?'

'She is over in Paris.'

'So I shall not see her again! That is a pity. I find your Sarah very simpatica. You will say au revoir to her for me, yes? Perhaps one day she will come to Berlin.'

It was not long after their conversation had dwindled into

a desultory exchange that Charles, to his considerable relief, heard the front-door bell ring. He got up and went across to the window. Drawing the curtain to one side, he peered down into the street.

'I think that must be someone to pick you up.'

Kurt jumped to his feet. His eyes were glistening with emotion as he clasped Charles' hand in both of his.

'Good-bye, my dear friend. We shall meet again. Do not come down.'

He turned suddenly flustered, it seemed, and ran out of the room so that Charles was still standing in the drawing-room when he heard the front-door slam.

What a macabre sort of evening it had been! But thank God it was over! He burnt with embarrassment when he contemplated his inept efforts at trying to solicit the truth from Kurt. It was all Wragg's fault. Wragg had tried to use him, just as he was sure that Kurt had used him. And he didn't like either of them for it.

As he walked across to the drink table to pour himself a nightcap, the telephone rang and he altered course to answer it.

'Mr. Ashmore?' He immediately recognized Wragg's clipped, dispassionate voice. 'I'm just phoning to say I'm on my way round to pick up Menke.'

CHAPTER XXIII

SARAH had been more relieved that she cared to reveal when Jerome Bowyer had returned to the flat soon after midnight.

The hours she had spent there alone had provided her with an opportunity to survey the day's events and her conclusion was that she must have been out of her mind to drop everything at a minute's notice and accompany him to Berlin. But though she was in Berlin, she wasn't out of her mind and she was forced to recognize that someone whom she thought she had worked out of her system was still able to blow her off course. It was no good pretending that it was the appeal to her sense of adventure which had been successful. The hard fact was that only Jerome Bowyer could have exercised such an influence over her. She wasn't in love with him any longer, she kept on telling herself, and yet he had this magnetic hold over her so that when he crooked his finger she ran. The shattering thing was to discover that she still did so after all this time. If anyone had suggested it up to eleven o'clock that morning, she'd have laughed in their face. But now here she was alone in a strange flat in Berlin with nothing to do but try and analyse the alchemy which had translated her there.

She had turned off the television soon after he had gone out. She couldn't understand the language and there was nothing remotely soothing in watching a play about a crippled woman, her thalidomide baby and her unfaithful husband.

Drink in hand, she had wandered about the flat trying to get some clue as to its owner's character. But at the end, she knew no more than Jerome Bowyer had told her, namely that it was owned by a woman friend whom he believed currently to be in Bangkok. She had had no compunction in opening drawers and cupboards in the hope of finding something interesting. But there was nothing. No photographs, not even a letter to provide a name. Two drawers in the desk over in one corner of the living-room were locked and she imagined there was probably a safe somewhere, but she hadn't yet reached the point of making a burglarious assault on the mysterious owner's property.

One thing which didn't surprise her was that Jerome Bowyer had a friend who owned such a flat and to which he had a key to come and go, apparently as he wanted. One of the reasons she had finally broken with him was because his life consisted of a series of secret compartments and you were never allowed to know what went on save in the one in which he had placed you.

While waiting for his return, she had spent a long time standing at the window staring out across the Tiergarten towards East Berlin. She found herself watching with fascination the S-Bahn trains silently worming their way to and from the eastern sector. It was the route which he had taken and she wondered where he was at that moment and what he was doing. Each time she reached this point, she would give a small shiver and turn away, only to be drawn back again a few minutes later to go through the same process once more.

It was just after midnight when she heard the front-door quietly open. She tiptoed across to the door of the living room and peered through the crack. To her relief, it was Jerome.

'I thought I heard the door,' she said in a nonchalant voice as she went out into the hall.

'Had a good evening?' he enquired as he took off his coat and threw it down on a chair.

'A very dull one.'

'Phone go at all?' he asked, fixing her with a quizzical look.'

'Only once. Not long after you left.'

He grinned. 'That was me. I just wanted to make sure you'd got the message. Good girl, you didn't answer.'

'Supposing I had?' she asked belligerently.

'I'd have given you hell.' He put an arm round her waist and guided her back into the living-room. 'I need a drink. What about you?'

'A Cointreau.'

'Good God, you haven't been drinking that all the evening, have you?'

'No, but I feel like one now.'

'So you've been bored?' he went on as he poured the drinks.

'Yes, but that's hardly surprising.'

'You never used to get bored.'

'How do you know how I feel when I'm alone?'

'But you're self-reliant like me.'

'Even self-reliant people can get bored.'

'I suppose so, but I thought you'd find things to interest you.'

'Such as?'

'Snooping around the flat for a start! Don't tell me you haven't made a good old search of the place.'

'Of course I have! But as you know, it didn't offer anything of interest.'

He gave a happy laugh. 'I'm afraid Eva doesn't leave much lying about when she goes away.'

'So her name is Eva?'

'Hadn't I told you that?'

'No. Only that she was in Bangkok.'

'It could be Phnom-Penh.'

'Just as her name could be Magdalena.'

He frowned. 'Why that name?' he asked in a suspicious tone.

'Aren't Eva and Magdalena the two female characters in Die Meistersinger?'

'Clever girl! But her name really is Eva.'

There was a silence, and then Sarah said, 'What sort of an evening have you had?'

'Useful.'

'Is that all you're going to say?'

He drained his glass and went back to the drink cabinet. When he returned to where she was sitting, he said, 'I'd sooner not talk about things this evening.'

She shrugged. 'I've been wondering why you wanted me to come. I'm still wondering.'

'Tomorrow.'

'We'll still be here tomorrow?'

'That's for sure.'

'And the day after?'

'That depends on tomorrow.'

Another silence fell. Eventually Sarah said, 'I think I'll go to bed.'

'Which room would you like?'

'The small one. I'd feel lost in Eva's bed.'

'It is a bit big for one person.'

'Then you'd better try and imagine that Eva's in it with you.'

He watched her leave the room, an amused smile on his face.

Sarah managed to go to sleep almost at once, but woke

up about an hour later. There was an unaccustomed sound coming from somewhere within the flat and she lifted her head off the pillow to listen. Someone was typing hard. Her watch showed two o'clock. She recalled occasions when Jerome Bowyer had worked right through a night and not shown any signs of it the next day. A few minutes later, she was asleep again.

When she next awoke, strong daylight was thrusting round the edge of the curtains. The bed was deliciously warm and for a time she just lay snuggling in its corrupting embrace, not wanting the day to advance any further.

There was a brief knock on her door and it opened to admit Jerome.

'I've brought you breakfast in bed,' he said, putting down a tray and going across to draw the curtains. 'You don't need to get up until you want to, but it's sunny, if cold, and I thought you might care to have a look around the city.'

Sarah propped herself up on one elbow and surveyed the tray. There was orange juice, coffee and some toast.

'That all right? I can do you an egg.'

'No, this is fine. I don't normally eat anything at all for breakfast.'

'I know you used not to,' he said with a knowing grin.

He was wearing a short, bright green towel bath-robe over a pair of canary yellow pyjamas. At least, he had on the bottom half of the pyjamas but not the top and Sarah remembered that this was his usual night attire in winter. In summer, he discarded the trousers as well.

He had obviously just shaved and there was a strong smell of a tangy lotion. As he stood smiling down at her, she was reminded of some brightly-coloured jungle bird, even to the amused glint in the eyes.

Without warning, he suddenly sat down on the bed and leant against her recumbent form, his face only inches from hers.

'I don't know what you have in mind,' she said evenly, 'but I can't eat breakfast with you like that.'

He laughed, and bending further forward kissed her on the lips. 'I always did like you first thing in the morning,' he remarked, after getting up and re-seating himself on the end of the bed.

'I heard you typing after I'd gone to bed last night,' Sarah remarked, aiming to say something devoid of emotional content.

'I thought I'd do my homework rather than leave it until today. I reckoned you'd be less than enchanted if I spent the whole of this morning at the typewriter.'

'I probably should have been. So what is the programme?'

'I'll show you some of the city.'

'And after that?'

'I have to go back to East Berlin.'

'What time?'

'I'll go about four o'clock. Earlier than yesterday, anyway.'

'Do I come with you?'

He shook his head. 'I'd like you to come, but it wouldn't be fair on anyone to suggest it.'

'I'm still wondering why you need me here at all.'

'Because if anything goes wrong this evening and I don't get back, you have the important task of taking my report back to London. That's what I was typing last night.'

'Where do I take it?'

'To head of section himself.'

'And tell him I accompanied you to Berlin and you've disappeared.'

'It's all in the report, anyway.'

'You're asking to be banished for ever.'

'If things go wrong this evening, I shall probably suffer a worse fate than being banished by my own chums. But the odds are they won't go wrong and I shall be able to report in person and no one will be any the wiser about Miss Sarah Ashmore having been brought out of retirement to play Pussy Galore to my James Bond.'

She put down her coffee cup, hoisted a pillow behind her head and resettled herself against it.

'What'll you be doing in East Berlin?'

'It's all in the report.'

'And the report is in a sealed envelope, I imagine?'

'Two, as a matter of fact.'

Sarah was thoughtful for a second. 'Look, Jerome, I want to know a bit more. I'm tired of being playfully teased. If you want me to co-operate in your plans, I insist upon being told more.'

'Or?'

'Or I'll fly back to London this morning and you can whistle up Eva from Phnom-Penh to be your courier.'

While she was speaking, the smile had remained fixed on his face but his eyes had gone glitter hard. She knew he was angry. He didn't like being thwarted, least of all by anyone whose compliance he was inclined to take for granted.

His voice was perfectly natural, however, when he spoke. He'd always had complete self-control of his emotion and it was only his eyes which indicated to those who could read the signs that his flow of adrenalin had increased.

'I have reason to believe that an agent in East Berlin is being held by the security police and I want to find out.'

'One of our agents?'

'Of course.'

'Does this have anything to do with Kurt Menke?'

'I believe so.'

'In what way?'

'Next question.'

'You mean you won't tell me?'

'I mean just that.'

'But you think you're on to the truth?'

'Yes, I do.' He paused and in a less stark tone went on, 'So much of our work is inference and reconstruction. All one can do is collect as many facts as possible and then set about drawing the right conclusion. It's very rare to be given the whole picture in one go.'

'And does Evelyn Ragnold have a part in the picture?'

'There are some who believe that Menke's defection is associated with Ragnold; there are others who doubt this.'

'Which category are you in?'

'The doubters, *now*.'

'But you could be wrong?'

'Certainly.'

'And it's all in your report?' she asked with a slow smile.

'It's all there.'

He edged up the bed and took her hand. 'I don't suppose you'd ever marry me?'

'Is that a proposal?'

'No, not really.'

'Then there's no point in answering it.'

'You mean you might say yes if I were serious?'

'No, not really.'

He ran a finger lightly up her forearm and back down to the palm of her hand. When he looked up at her, he was wearing his little boy expression.

'May I?'

'May you what?'

'Get into bed with you?'

'No.'

'Why not?'

'Because I don't want you to. Because it's not what I came to Berlin to do. Admittedly I don't seem to have come for very much, but that's definitely not on the agenda.'

'But the very fact you came at all shows that you——you still have feelings towards me.'

'Possibly, but I'm not sure what those feelings are.'

'Let's find out.'

'Not that way.'

'Is that your final answer?'

'It is.'

'Then there's nothing left for me to do but go and wash up the breakfast things.' He leaned quickly forward and kissed her again before she could move. Then picking up her breakfast tray he went out of the room humming quietly to himself.

For a few minutes, Sarah lay propped against the pillows, wishing furiously that she had never come—that Jerome Bowyer had never re-entered her life. She had a wild urge to fling on her clothes and run all the way to the airport to catch the first plane home. It was not that she was angry with him, just that he made for so many complications.

In the event, however, she took a long time getting dressed and it was eleven o'clock before she emerged from the bedroom. Jerome was sitting reading in the living-room. He looked up and gave her a smile as she entered.

'Ready?'

'Yes. Sorry if I've been a long time.'

'There's no hurry. We'll get a taxi and go down to the Kurfüstendamm. That's the starting-point for seeing West Berlin.'

Sarah had expected that the day might prove something of a strain, but, with Jerome in one of his moods of sunny charm, it flew by as she quickly reacted to the spell of his company.

They returned to the flat at three o'clock after an excellent lunch.

'I'll be off shortly,' he said in a businesslike voice, which was as different from the voice on their outing as a crack of thunder from a soughing breeze. He handed her an envelope. 'Put this in your handbag and give it back to me on my return. Failing my return, take it to London by the first plane tomorrow and hand it personally to head of section.' He grinned suddenly. 'Don't try and steam the envelope open because you won't be able to. It's one of our specials.' He picked up his coat off a chair and put it on, patting the pocket to make sure Mr. Sean O'Riordan's passport was there. 'I'd sooner you didn't go out, even if it is boring for you here.' He glanced round the room, at the bookshelves and the hi-fi record player. 'You could be much worse off. And remember not to answer the phone if it rings.' He turned to go. 'See you later tonight, I hope.'

A second later he had gone, leaving Sarah reflecting on the number of different Jerome Bowyers who paraded around in a single skin. This last one hadn't even given her a peck on the cheek as he set out on a hazardous mission. But he always had been disconcertingly single-minded.

There were only two points of entry for a foreigner to pass from West into East Berlin. There was Checkpoint Charley where you could enter by car or on foot and the Friedrichstrasse Station which you could reach by S-Bahn, as Jerome had done the previous evening, or by U-Bahn, the Berlin underground railway, one of whose lines serving West Berlin passed beneath the eastern sector with the trains making a stop at Friedrichstrasse Station before careering on through several ghostly, shuttered stations and regaining the west.

Before setting out, he had toyed with the idea of entering through Checkpoint Charley, but didn't wish to take a car and his previous experiences had taught him that, though there wasn't much in it, the formalities were liable to be more protracted than Friedrichstrasse Station. And as Sean O'Riordan was unlikely to be recognized or remembered from the earlier evening, there was no harm in once more going in that way. Not that it very much mattered if he were remembered. A lot of foreigners paid several visits to East Berlin—provided they had the stamina.

Nevertheless, he decided to go by U-Bahn, even though he would end up in the same dreary limbo on arrival at Friedrichstrasse Station. The only difference being that tonight he would ascend to it where last night he had descended.

He walked to Hansaplatz underground station and took a northbound train to Leopoldplatz. There he changed to a different line and caught a train going south to Tempelhof.

The first two stations were still in West Berlin. But shortly after leaving the second, the train slowed and an air vent covered by wire indicated that they had arrived beneath East Berlin. There were three stations before Friedrichstrasse, each of them dimly-lit, with barricaded exits and revealing an armed policeman lurking in the shadows on the platform. The train slowed down to pass through these ghost stations in a way that reminded Jerome of tip-toeing through a graveyard at night so as not to disturb the spirits.

And then came Friedrichstrasse Station where he and two other passengers alighted. He made his way up to ground level and to the dismal room with its welcoming posters, its stern-faced officials and throng of bewildered inmates waiting to be admitted to the capital of the D.D.R.

On this occasion, the unsmiling Vopo on duty was a good-looking lad of not more than nineteen or twenty. But his instructions could well have been to belie the benign and friendly posters on the walls.

After the inevitable delay during which bureaucratic protocol was being grimly served somewhere behind the partitions, Jerome retrieved his passport, satisfied the customs official that he was carrying nothing subversive and emerged into the open air.

On this occasion, he decided against taking a taxi as he didn't wish to run the risk of being remembered. Instead he walked round to the farther side of the station and used 20 pfennigs of the East German currency he had been obliged to acquire to buy a ticket on the S-Bahn to Alexanderplatz. There he changed to the U-Bahn and took a train to the penultimate station on the line.

The previous evening he had travelled to the last station, but once more caution dictated a change. It was just possible that an observant official would recall the face of an obvious stranger. The farther you left behind the busy centres of a city, the more conspicuous a visitor was liable to become.

Darkness was falling as he stepped out of the Station and a bitter east wind gave him the excuse of turning up his coat collar around his ears and lowering his head so that his features became less identifiable. He was grateful to the wind not only for providing him with the excuse, but for discouraging anyone from being interested in anything apart from reaching the shelter of their homes.

He turned into the street where V's flat lay, some way from the building in which it was situated so that he could keep it under observation the whole distance of his approach. It had a lonely, desolate air and there was nothing to arouse his suspicion.

Frau Koch's reaction to his enquiries the previous evening had convinced him that his visit would have been quickly reported to the police. Her clumsy insistence that he should return the next evening as Herr Grisinger would otherwise be so disappointed at missing him was clearly part of a plan. He now had no doubt that V had been arrested and his mother, if not also arrested, whisked out of the way. Meanwhile the neighbours had been warned to report any interest in the missing occupants of flat 16.

The question was what sort of reception was being

planned for his second visit! By arriving several hours early, he hoped to discover and to be able to put together the pieces which would provide a clue to V's fate.

Of course it was possible that they had reckoned on this and that he was even at this moment being drawn into a subtly baited trap. He shrugged inside the warmth of his coat. An exercise of this sort was always like treading a path through a minefield. You couldn't eliminate the danger, all you could do was try and anticipate it. If you failed, it was one up to the other side. Jerome Bowyer smiled to himself. Despite the blood-congealing wind, he could feel his adrenalin starting to course.

He had previously noticed that the building opposite V's was empty and shuttered, presumably awaiting demolition. If he could get inside there, he would have an excellent observation post. It was a corner site and he would not only be able to watch the whole of the front of V's block, but the adjacent cross roads as well.

As he approached the empty building, he slackened his pace only imperceptibly. Then quickly glancing around to make sure he himself was not being watched, he slid into the darkened doorway and flattened himself against the rough wooden planks which shuttered the entrance.

Where there's a deserted building, there, usually, children have been playing and the erosion of termites is as nothing compared with their destructive burrowings.

He ran his hand over the planks behind his back. Yes, one of them was loose. With a little pressure it swung inwards. He had a small rodent-like smile as he slithered through the narrow space, and then quickly shoving the plank back into position, he froze against the wall and listened hard. Somewhere overhead water was slowly dripping at the rate of one drip every five seconds. Otherwise all was silent.

Cautiously he tried his weight on the floorboards. They seemed intact, though littered with debris. He would wait a few minutes until his eyes had become accustomed to the dark inside the building.

He heard a car go by outside, but, to his relief, it didn't stop. He didn't want anything to start happening until he was ready and he was now confident that he had arrived before the other side.

After a few minutes, he left his listening post. On the right was a doorway leading into a large room which had boarded up windows facing on to both streets. Light from the street lamp on the corner outside filtered through the cracks and gave the room an eerie appearance. There was a sudden paper-scuffling noise over in the far corner of the room as a rat scurried away from the unwelcome intruder.

But Jerome had no wish to infringe its rights, being set on finding the staircase and installing himself in the room above, if that were possible.

The staircase turned out to be round a corner at the end of the passage. Before venturing up, he squatted down and ran a hand over the bottom three stairs. They seemed quite firm, though the bannister beside them had gone, probably removed for firewood by someone.

He ascended slowly, bent low, and using his hands as feelers to warn him of dangers head. But he reached the top without mishap and groped his way towards the front of the building. There were two doorways on his left leading into small rooms and then came a third which led into the front room on this floor. By now he realized that the large room below ran the length of the three rooms on the floor above.

He entered the room and was delighted to find that it, too, had windows facing two directions. First he examined the one looking out across the street at the building in which V lived. It was crudely boarded up and he had no difficulty in dislodging one of the pieces of timber so as to improve his line of vision. Next he did the same thing at the other window, though in wrenching away a slat of wood there was a sudden sound like a crack of thunder and he stood appalled by the noise he had caused. Reassured that no one had heard, or if they had had not thought twice of it (the malevolent wind was once more on his side making its own contribution to noises off) he set off to reconnoitre possible lines of retreat should departure by the same way as he had entered become impracticable for any reason.

By the time he returned to the front room, he had decided that, if the worst came to the worst, he would have to go up another two floors, climb out on to a small flat roof, across a parapet to the building next door and then just hope he would be able to make his way down to what looked like a builder's yard. It might well be that he would then find himself neatly trapped anyway, so he'd best hope to be able to leave as he had entered.

During his exploration he found a bucket and he carried this back to the room with him. It would provide something to sit on and, in an emergency, it could become quite a handy weapon. He remembered with what satisfactory results he had once before clouted somebody with an old-fashioned galvanized bucket. He had swung it in a hundred and eighty degrees arc and caught his adversary on the side of the head, felling him like a pole-axed ox. He grinned as he also had the agreeable vision of ramming the bucket hard over an unsuspecting head.

For two hours he sat gazing out intently at the building opposite and the street below. Anyone other than Jerome Bowyer might have become bored and dispirited, but he had never minded these long vigils. While he watched, he recited chunks of Swinburne quietly to himself.

There were no lights in the windows of V's flat and only three people came or went during that time. Two of them middle-aged women and one a youth with his right leg in a caliper.

And then just after seven o'clock, a small saloon car drew up a few yards past the entrance and two men got out. They had on heavy overcoats which reached below their shins and each was wearing a wide-brimmed felt hat turned down in front.

One of them crossed the street to Jerome's side and was lost to view. The other walked a few yards to the junction, looked all about him and strolled back to the car which he re-entered. Jerome noticed that it had a tall aerial at the rear.

He moved across to the other window and was in time to see other unmistakable figures standing in postures of studied nonchalance. There were four of them, each heavily overcoated, two of them wearing the familiar velour felt hats beloved of East German officialdom and the other two in fur hats. As he watched them, they took up positions in doorways and melted from his view.

By the time he returned to the first window, the car had driven off and there was no sign of either of the men.

He squatted back on the upturned bucket to await events, exhilarated that he had not misjudged the situation. Something was certainly about to happen and he, the obvious object of the sudden activity, was going to have a grandstand view.

His exhilaration was short-lived, however, when sounds from below told him that others had also decided to use the deserted building as a convenient observation post.

Voices floated up and he was puzzled, after surviving his initial shock, to discover how easily he could hear the voices of two men who were conversing. They were obviously in the large room beneath and if he could hear them so clearly, it meant that any movement on his part must be equally audible, if not more so.

He noticed a faint glow over in one corner of the room and peered anxiously in the direction. Then he realized that it was where a radiator pipe must have gone through the floor to the room below. The pipe had been ripped out and had left a hole through which the men's voices were being relayed.

Moving with catlike stealth, he edged his way towards the hole.

'Better put out your torch,' one of the men said, and the glow of light was promptly extinguished. 'You keep watch out of that side window and I'll stay at this one.'

'I think I heard a rat,' the other man said. He had a younger voice and Jerome imagined he was the subordinate of the one who had just given the orders.

'The place is probably alive with them,' the first man replied unsympathetically.

'And the draught is killing.'

'What did you think you were coming on, a summer picnic?'

'There's no need to be sarcastic. Hans has the best job, sitting in the car. I bet old Hans hasn't got a draught whistling round his balls.'

140

Jerome's smile broadened as the older man said with a harsh chuckle, 'You'd better watch out or the rats'll get yours. There was a farmer near Magdeburg who had his bitten off some years ago.'

'Both of them, for God's sake?'

'Natürlich, our East German rats are world leaders when it comes to sport.'

'You're joking?'

'Undo your trousers and see.'

'What happened to the farmer?'

'His wife divorced him.' Another harsh chuckle accompanied the remark, after which a silence fell below.

There had been nothing particularly fortifying in the earthy exchange, but Jerome had enjoyed it while it lasted. It showed that even East German security police had a human side when they didn't think anyone was around.

'Wonder if he'll turn up?' the younger one said, breaking the silence.

'He's not due for another hour.'

'Hope he comes. I shall like to see him walk into our net.'

'Ssh, something's happening now!'

Jerome swivelled round on his bucket to look out of the window again. A car had drawn up outside the apartment block opposite. From the rear door on the farther side three men got out. Or perhaps it might be truer to say that the man in the middle was bundled out between the other two, who hurried him inside the building. But Jerome had had no difficulty in recognizing V.

A few minutes later, lights appeared in V's flat and one of the men came across to the window and drew the curtains. Meanwhile the car had driven off and the street assumed its normal, deserted air, save that, as he now knew, every approach was covered by watchful eyes. Eyes skinned and alerted to his arrival.

He allowed himself to slump into a more comfortable posture in the knowledge that activity was certainly over for the time being.

His fears about V were confirmed. He was under arrest and being used as human bait in the trap which they had set to catch the mysterious visitor who had tried to get in touch with him the previous night.

He glanced at his watch. They would be expecting him to arrive in about three quarters of an hour. His approach would be observed and signalled ahead. He would be allowed to reach the flat and he had no doubt that V himself would open the door. There was no other point in having brought him there. They would hope, of course, that he would give himself away when he saw V. At all events, the closing of the front door would be the snapping to of the trap and he would find himself under arrest. In the circumstances, Sean O'Riordan's passport would certainly prove a damaging liability. But as there was no question of his walking into the trap, it didn't matter.

During the next hour, silence reigned, apart from the occasional exchange of comment below. For them, the critical time was approaching, as they believed. The knock-up was over, the match was on in earnest.

Jerome managed to forget about their presence as his mind became totally occupied with the implications of V's arrest.

Another hour went by before he reckoned he had fitted together enough of the pieces to know what had happened. Inevitably there were gaps in his knowledge, but intelligent guesswork bridged these.

When he finally alighted on what he was now certain must be the truth, he was filled with a bursting sense of frustration that there was nothing he could do. He couldn't even safely cry out 'Eureka'.

He wondered how long they would give him before deciding he wasn't going to turn up. At least a couple of hours if not longer. It might be twelve o'clock before the watch was called off which would mean he couldn't get back to West Berlin until tomorrow morning as the S-Bahn shut down at midnight.

And time was now of the essence.

The two men below began to talk again and he moved to where he could hear them better. It was possible that he might learn something of their intentions.

'Doesn't look as if he's coming,' the younger one said.

'Have patience.'

'There's a woman approaching. I wonder if it's her?'

'We're waiting for a man.'

'But it might be a woman this time.'

'It'll be a man.'

'She's crossed over and gone into a house.'

'I told you.'

'It's crazy when we don't even know who to look out for.'

'We'll know soon enough. Anyway we've got a description.'

'About thirty-five, fair hair, spare build, blue eyes.' The younger one's tone was scornful.

'We also know his name. Pick.'

'He's probably using a different one tonight.'

'All the better for us. Proves he's up to no good.'

'What's this Grisinger supposed to have done?'

'Betrayed the homeland.'

'How?'

'I don't know and one doesn't ask.'

'I've no time for traitors.'

'Who has!'

'Where did he work?'

'In a liaison section with the Soviet K.G.B.'

The younger one digested this piece of information in silence for a time.

'He must have been important.'

'A small cog in an important machine.'

'How did they get on to him?'

'I don't know. Anyway, you ask too many questions.'

'I'm just interested.'

'It's not wise to be too interested. You should know that.'

'I'm sure he's not coming now. How much longer do you think they'll keep us here?'

'I don't know.'

'Surely not all night?'

'Somebody may have to remain here all night.'

'Not us?'

'I don't know.'

'We'll freeze to death.'

'They'll bring us hot soup.'

'I'd much sooner go home.'

'That's the trouble of having a young wife.'

'How do you mean?'

'She takes your mind off your duty.'

'Ilse's a loyal party member.'

'She's still a woman.'

'She's good, too.' The young one's voice was wistful and full of appreciation. 'Good in bed, I mean.'

'Better mind out those rats don't get you then, or she'll divorce you like the farmer's wife!' There was a pause, then the older man said, 'Go and have a look around upstairs.'

'Why?'

'There might be better positions than here, particularly if we're going to be here all night.'

'Why don't we both go?'

'Idiot! Someone must keep watch.' After a further pause, 'Well, go on, or are you afraid?'

'Who's afraid?'

'I think you are. You're afraid a rat might gnaw off one of your balls.'

'I'd still be better with one than a lot of men are with two.' The tone was engagingly defiant and Jerome smiled grimly to himself as he reflected that there were worse fates than rat bites awaiting anyone who ventured up to the first floor.

He had already risen to his feet and was holding the bucket in his right hand.

'Here take my torch, but careful how you use it.'

Jerome tiptoed across to the door and took up a position from where he would be able to swing the bucket into action as soon as anyone appeared.

He heard the man move along the passage and begin to mount the stairs. He was flashing the torch freely about him obviously bent on frightening off rats and any other lurking dangers.

Though ready for action, Jerome hoped fervently that it wouldn't become necessary. The noise was bound to bring up the older man and heaven knows where it might all end. It was an occasion when discretion was certainly the better part of valour.

144

The torch-bearer had reached the top of the stairs and was directing the beam along the passage which ran outside the room where Jerome was waiting. He heard him move a pace closer and could tell that he was now shining the torch into the first of the three rooms. The man was breathing heavily and it was not difficult for Jerome to imagine that he could also hear his heart pounding. He had reduced his own breathing to a point where the rise and fall of his chest was imperceptible.

He judged that the man had just reached the second doorway and shone his torch through when there was a furious sound of small, scuttering feet and the beam of light danced about crazily in the passage outside. At the same time the man gave a strangulated gasp.

For one moment, Jerome wondered whether the grim prophecies of his companion below hadn't been fulfilled, but then he heard a hurried retreat being beaten back down the stairs and he relaxed.

'Well?' It was the voice of the older man.

'No, this is better.'

'Did you look properly?'

'Of course.'

'Meet any rats?'

'Only one and I sent him packing.'

'I bet!'

'I did. Anyway, if you don't believe me, you go and have a look upstairs and I'll keep watch down here.'

'I may have to later.'

A short time after this, Jerome heard a quiet knocking on one of the barricaded windows below, followed by the sound of voices.

'What's happening?' the younger one asked eagerly a few seconds later.

'It's being called off.'

'For all of us?'

'Yes. Someone's being left up in the flat, but otherwise it's over.'

'Well, I'm sorry we didn't catch the bastard. Bet he looked nothing like the description. Blue eyes, indeed!'

About ten minutes later, a car drew up opposite, and V

was hurried out and driven away. The lights in his flat re-mained on, however, confirming that someone had been left just in case Jerome should still put in an appearance.

It was another half hour before further activity outside indicated that the various observers were being withdrawn. The two below Jerome made quite a noise getting out and he stood up in an attempt to see what they looked like. After four hours of their company he had formed pictures of each in his mind's eye.

For a couple of minutes they stood together on the edge of the pavement and then a car came up and they got in.

The older one was as he had imagined him. Generally square in shape and with close-cropped dark hair which was revealed when he suddenly removed his hat to scratch his head. The young one had high cheek bones and a full mouth and was slim by comparison with his companion. He was wearing a shiny black leather coat and a jaunty-looking cap of similar material. He had blonde hair which clustered thickly in the nape of his neck.

Jerome was intrigued. His dress and appearance were so different from the ordinary run of the security police that he didn't seem to belong; yet he obviously did. Perhaps he had been groomed for the role of sexual compriser. If so, he had presumably been press-ganged into service this evening be-cause of a shortage of other officers. That would account for his chattiness and, at the same time, his absence of routine respect for the older man; also the other's slightly taunting attitude towards him. Yes, that must be it, the younger one had merely been on loan from another branch of the service.

He glanced at his watch. It was twenty minutes to mid-night, which meant he would have to remain in East Berlin until the next morning when the trains began running again.

It was a frustrating prospect, but he had learnt to control most of his emotions for most of the time, including his sense of frustration.

He decided that, uncomfortable as it was, he had better stay where he was, at least until about five o'clock. It was tempting to leave now, but there were obvious dangers in moving from one all-night café to another; and he wasn't even sure if there were any. The last thing he wanted was to draw attention to himself and it was difficult not to do this in a communist city where life shuts down early and the only persons abroad are the very ones you wish to avoid.

He comforted himself with the thought that he would still be back at the flat before Sarah left. With this, he moved the bucket over to a corner of the room, sat down and wedged himself into the right angle and went to sleep.

He awoke several times in the course of the night, cold and stiff, which gave him the excuse to get up and peer out through the cracks in the boarded up windows. But there was never any sign of activity and he noticed that the light in the front room of V's flat had been extinguished. Not that that meant it was now empty.

Shortly before five o'clock he decided to leave. He crept downstairs, loosened the plank in the doorway and squeezed through. Before stepping out on to the pavement, he glanced cautiously in both directions. It was the hour when the first workmen were sallying forth and he didn't wish to bump into one right outside V's flat.

When he judged it was safe to leave the cover of the doorway, he scuttled off like one of the rats he had left behind, hugging the wall with an animal's natural protective instinct.

After twelve hours of being cooped up in circumstances of great personal peril, he found it an enormous relief to be indulging in uninhibited physical movement again. He would steer himself towards the Frankfurterallee, which became the Karl Marx allee as it got closer to the heart of East Berlin, and walk westwards. The U-Bahn ran beneath that street and he could dive into one of the stations when he felt like it.

Though the wind had dropped a bit, it was still an extremely cold morning, with an occasional spit of icy rain. He passed a cafe, its windows steamed up from the presence of half a dozen muffled figures bent over cups of coffee. He longed to join them, but realized that the appearance of a stranger in their midst at this hour of the morning would inevitably arouse interest.

By six o'clock he had reached the Alexanderplatz. Another half hour and he'd be at Friedrichstrasse Station. The walk had brought him to physical life again and he decided to continue and have a cup of coffee there before passing through the controls and taking the S-Bahn into West Berlin.

It was while he was walking along Unter den Linden towards its junction with Friedrichstrasse that a disagreeable thought entered his head. The police had his description, albeit it fitted a hundred others, and might well be on the look-out for someone of his general appearance. That could lead to questions and he would have to rely on Sean O'Riordan bluffing his way past.

What on earth was he doing wearing the same coat as he'd worn the first time! Besides giving the police his physical description, Frau Koch would certainly have mentioned what he was wearing and his suede coat could scarcely have been missed.

He turned abruptly to his left and dived down beside the Opera House, crossed over the Französischestrasse and entered that part of East Berlin which had been the heart of the undivided city and which now stood as a reminder of what war had done to Berlin. It was a wasteland of derelict sites and grim, unusable buildings.

He was now heading towards the wall which ran east and west not more than a quarter of a mile in front.

He had reckoned that there wouldn't be a soul about and there wasn't. After a quick glance about him, he shot behind the wall of a bombed out building and, removing his coat, thrust it behind a pile of rubble.

When he got back on to the deserted street, he turned up his jacket collar, gave himself a quick brush down and set off for Friedrichstrasse Station.

By now there were a fair number of people about in the area of the station and he made his way straight to the control point.

The uniformed official took his passport and examined it with meticulous care. Then he looked up at Jerome and said in German, 'Where have you been all night?'

'Nix understand,' Jerome said apologetically. With a sheepish grin, he added, 'Ich komm—komm, yes?—Ich komm yesterday nacht. I have good time in your city.' He put on a rueful expression. 'Too much cognac.' He clasped his head. 'I miss last train. Understand? Verstanden?'

'Doch, ich verstehe.' He was a middle-aged man with an amused twinkle in his eye. 'Es gibt viele Vernügen in Berlin, ja?'

Jerome nodded eagerly as it was clearly the expected response. Many pleasures in Berlin, indeed!

A couple of minutes later, Sean O'Riordan was on his way to the platform from which left the S-Bahn trains to the west.

Sarah was in the kitchen when he arrived back at the flat. She was so absorbed in watching the coffee pot bubbling that she didn't hear him enter. In fact, her mind was in something of a turmoil after a night in which every small sound had brought her sitting bolt upright. Jerome's failure to return had finally knocked her off balance. Despite what he had said, she had been quite confident that he would reappear around midnight. She had sat up until two and then gone to bed still sure that he would be back before morning. At half past six she had risen and gone and sat in the living-room, staring, as though hypnotized, towards the eastern sector.

Finally, when all hope of his return had faded, she had drifted into the kitchen to make coffee.

'That's just what I need,' he said in a matter-of-fact tone after watching her in silence for a few seconds.

She started and turned. 'You're back!' Relief showed in every feature, not least in her voice.

He gave her one of his looks of detached amusement. 'I'm just going into the bathroom, then I'll be with you. Incidentally, are you ready to leave?'

'I haven't packed yet.'

'Do it now. We'll be going in about half an hour. We can get a plane to Dusseldorf and a connecting flight from there. I don't want to miss it, so don't stand about.'

'Jerome Bowyer, you are quite the most infuriating, self-centred person who ever trod this planet.' But before she

149

was half-way through, she found herself addressing an empty doorway.

It didn't take her more than a few minutes to throw her things into a case and when she returned to the kitchen, he was already there, standing by the stove, cup in hand.

'You look as though you've had a rough time. Did it go all right?'

He nodded. 'There were one or two dodgy moments, but I'm back safely and I discovered what I set out to discover. It's now a question of getting back to London as quickly as possible. We can be there by lunchtime if we don't miss the plane.'

'If you miss it, it won't be on my account,' she replied in a nettled tone.

His face suddenly broke into a grin. 'You're still a great girl. I know I'm impossible, but then you know it, too.' He came across and kissed her as she stood just inside the door. 'Now it's time to go. Ready?'

CHAPTER XXIV

WRAGG had been up all night, which had done nothing to improve his temper. Menke's escape was unforgivable. It was no use saying that it was all due to bad luck, because it wasn't. Part of it was due to the most inexcusable of all errors in his particular line of business: an under-estimation of the opponent.

He had envisaged the possibility of Menke attempting to abscond and had laid plans accordingly. Charles Ashmore's house had been kept under surveillance the whole time Menke was inside. There'd even been a man watching the back in case he should make a getaway through the lavatory window, down a drainpipe and over the wall which ran at the bottom of the small garden.

When Menke had made his hurried exit from the house

and got into the Skoda car which had drawn up outside, Wragg's own two men had set off in pursuit. Confident—and this was the inexcusable part—that the occupants of the Skoda had no idea that they were being shadowed.

The car had been driven at a sedate pace up Edgware Road, had turned east along St John's Wood Road before heading north again in the direction of Swiss Cottage. They reached Finchley Road and the thing had become a piece of cake, when, without warning, the Skoda, which had been meticulous about observing the traffic lights, suddenly accelerated across a set which had just turned red and went on accelerating until it was quickly lost to sight. Wragg's men who had allowed another car to get between them and the Skoda found themselves stuck behind this car until the lights turned green, by which time the Skoda could have been on Mars for all they could do about it.

When the news reached Wragg, the miasma of his anger had sent people reeling out of the building for fresh air.

He had immediately had Menke's description circulated to all exit points, with a special warning to Special Branch officers at Heathrow and at the channel ports. He had also demanded details of any ship in the Port of London which was flying the flag of an East European country.

Meanwhile, he had discovered that the Skoda was registered in the name of an assistant defence attaché at the Czech Embassy. The attaché himself lived in a flat on Campden Hill with his wife and one child. He had the flat placed under immediate surveillance, but called this off when he learnt, just as dawn was breaking, that the attaché and his family had returned to Prague two weeks previously. The new owner of the car had not been notified to the authorities.

All he could now do was sit back and wait—and initiate new lines of enquiry if he could think of any.

Brigstock, to whom he had reported the dismal slip-up as soon as it had happened, was not coming into the office before lunchtime as he had a morning meeting at the Ministry of Defence. However, he phoned just after eight o'clock when Wragg was on his umpteenth cup of coffee. The conversation was terse and unproductive. Towards the end, Brigstock said, 'Let's hope he doesn't suddenly pop up in someone's embassy and hold a press conference.'

'I can't see how that would help him.'

'Nevertheless, let's hope he doesn't.'

'He's much more likely to be smuggled out.'

'And we still don't know why he ever came in.'

'I'll get through to Bowyer's head of section as soon as he's in his office.'

'You've still some time to wait. He's never in until after ten. Anyway, phone me if anything breaks. I can always slip out of my meeting. And you'd better put the D.G. in the picture as soon as he arrives.'

'Yes,' Wragg said, without enthusiasm.

It was about an hour later that his phone rang and a voice identified itself as belonging to Bowyer's section.

'I've got a message for you from Jerome Bowyer. It's a bit cryptic. It reads: "Inform Wragg on my way back. Case solved. Hold everything, especially our friend." It probably makes more sense to you than to me. I gather he'll be back by middle day.'

Case solved indeed! A typical piece of Bowyer arrogance. 'Hold everything, especially our friend.' At that moment Wragg was close to hoping that Jerome Bowyer's plane would crash. When towards the end of the morning, Bowyer phoned from Heathrow to say that he would be with him within the hour. Wragg felt obliged to mention that Menke had disappeared. Bowyer's comment made him then wish that the plane had actually crashed.

CHAPTER XXV

SARAH waited until she reached her flat before telephoning her father, only to be told by Miss Acres that he had gone out to lunch a few minutes earlier. She ascertained that he was not lunching with anyone which meant that he wouldn't be out very long. On such occasions he usually ate in the snack bar of his club and unless he happened to meet an old friend he hadn't seen for a long time, he was usually back in his office soon after two.

On this reckoning and allowing him a few minutes' grace, Sarah phoned again at two-fifteen and was immediately put through.

'I thought I'd just let you know I was back, daddy. If you're free, may I come and eat with you this evening?'

'I can't think of anything I'd enjoy more. We'll go out and celebrate.'

'I'd sooner eat at home if that's all right.'

'Certainly. What's the trouble, have you been over-indulging in Paris?'

'No, it's not that. It's just that I want to talk to you.'

'Nothing wrong, is there?' he enquired in a worried voice.

'No, but I've got things to tell you and it'll be quieter at home.'

'All right, darling, come round as early as you like. I shall be back by six.'

'I'll probably be waiting for you.'

'You're sure nothing's wrong?'

'Promise. It's just that I've got things to tell you. Incidentally, I was sorry to hear about Evelyn Ragnold.'

'Oh, you know about that?'

'Yes, I saw an English paper. Have they established the cause of death yet?'

'As a matter of fact, I heard this morning. He died of a broken neck as a direct result of the car crash.'

'That's definite?'

'They're still carrying out tests on various organs, but that's only because Wragg's lot are so damned suspicious and never want to believe the obvious.'

'You must be relieved that it was a genuine accident.'

'I didn't say quite that.'

'Quite what?'

'That it was a genuine accident.'

'I don't understand——'

'Wragg's convinced that it was a serious attempt to free Ragnold.'

153

'And you also believe that?'

'I think it's very possible.'

'And he was killed by accident?'

'Yes.'

'That makes his death rather ironic.'

'I agree. Incidentally, Kurt has disappeared, but I'll tell you about that this evening.'

It was only after he had rung off that he realized she had failed to make any comment on his final bit of news, which was surprising, when he thought about it.

In the event he left the office earlier than he had intended and was home soon after half past five. Even so, Sarah was already there.

She jumped up as he entered the drawing-room and came across to kiss him on both cheeks.

'Not been working this afternoon?' She shook her head. 'When did you get back?'

'Just before lunch. And it wasn't Paris I've been to. It was Berlin.' The words came out in a rush and continued as she related the events of the previous forty-eight hours.

When she finished, her father was silent for a time, then he said with a rueful smile, 'I'm glad I didn't know what was happening.'

'Even if I could have told you, I'm not sure I would have. You seemed to have enough cares about your head.'

'And this chap Bowyer thinks he's on to the truth?'

'He's sure of it.'

'But he wouldn't tell you what it was?'

'No.'

'I imagine Kurt's disappearance will have come as something of a surprise to him?'

Sarah made a face. 'I don't think he and Wragg had very warm feelings towards each other before.'

'And you say Bowyer doesn't believe that Menke's defection and Ragnold's trial were connected in any way?'

'I gathered not.'

'Wragg's convinced they are.'

'Jerome Bowyer isn't infallible.' His daughter's tone caused Charles to glance at her sharply.

'He may not be infallible, but he obviously exercises a strong influence over some people.'

'I wish he'd never come back into my life,' Sarah burst out.

'There's no need for you to see him again now that everything's more or less over.'

She nodded unhappily. 'He's the only man I've ever met who has this hold over me. I thought I'd got over it, but obviously I hadn't.'

'It sounds like a love–hate relationship.'

'If love means losing your will power and hate means resenting the fact, then that's what it is.' She paused before adding firmly, 'What it *was*.' She paused again and said, 'Which is a great shame, because he really can be tremendous fun to be with. He's such a stimulating sort of person.'

'Mrs. Burden won't have started to cook yet,' Charles said in a judicious voice, 'so why don't we go out to dinner? I think it's in both our interests not only to relax in a pleasant restaurant but to absent ourselves from the telephone for an evening. Either Jerome Bowyer or the ineffable Wragg is sure to phone. Probably both of them!'

CHAPTER XXVI

KURT Menke looked up expectantly as he heard voices outside the door. It opened and the larger of the two men who had roughed up him and Charles on Chanctonbury Ring came in.

He walked over to Kurt, who stood up, and clapped his hands against Kurt's shoulders in salutation.

'I am sorry, my friend, that I have not been to see you yet, but I have been busy all day with arrangements for your return.'

'When?'

'Tomorrow night. But first let us drink to success.'

155

They spoke in English which was their only common language.

The big man stood back and surveyed Kurt's features. 'It is good. No marks left. It is not nice to attack a friend, but we had to make a good pretence, yes? Your English friend, he did not suspect anything?'

'No, it was not difficult for him to believe that my life was in danger.'

'Good, good! It has gone well, our scheme.' He walked to the door and called out, 'Mikhail, I told you to bring us drink.'

The man, who had been attending to Kurt's needs since his arrival at the house the previous evening, appeared with a bottle of vodka and two glasses. The big man took them from him and closed the door.

'You have been comfortable here?'

Kurt nodded. 'I shall be glad to get home.'

'That is natural. And you have deserved well.' He filled the glasses and handed one to Kurt.

'Bottoms up, as they say here.'

'Prosit.'

'Here, some more. It is good on a cold night.'

'What have you arranged?'

'Presently, I tell you.'

Kurt sat down without taking his eyes off the other man. He felt on edge. Twenty-four hours cooped up in a single room in a house somewhere on the outskirts of London without being told anything had brought him to a stage of fidgeting tension.

But the big man seemed to be in a relaxed mood and to be in no hurry to disclose the plans which had been made to get Kurt out of the country. He gave a reminiscent chuckle.

'It was good that rendezvous on Chanctonbury Ring on a British Sunday afternoon. It was artistic, that arrangement. And Wragg suspected nothing either?'

'Wragg suspected everything all the time.'

The big man gave an explosive laugh. 'To be too suspicious brings its own dangers. It was very good that he believed you were come for Ragnold. You played that very well, my friend.'

'Once we knew the Ragnold trial was to be held and we learnt that Charles Ashmore was his lawyer, the timetable arranged itself. The important thing was to lay a false trail and Ragnold was perfect for such a purpose.'

'Yes, yes, he was a fine red herring, as they call it here.' He put on an expression of mock sorrow. 'But now he is a dead red herring. It is funny that they think we killed him, when we were only presenting a little diversion. We pretend to try and free him and he ends up dead. It is lucky that we did not need him any more. Incidentally, our two men made sure they got away without being identified.'

Kurt smiled for the first time. It was a small, complacent smile. 'And they never did guess the real reason for my defection. To catch a traitor!'

'Grisinger's days of betrayal are over! Soon all his days will be over!' The big man's voice was harsh.

'Perhaps he ought to have been caught before, but it always is difficult with such people. You know that somewhere in your organization there is a leak, that information is being passed to the enemy, but to identify the culprit is a different matter.'

'You have done well, my friend, to unmask this traitor. You can tell me now, who thought out the plan which has brought Grisinger to his downfall?'

'The head of our section. Only he and I knew the whole plan. Grisinger was allowed to find out that I was to make a false defection, but, of course he did not know the true reason, which was to trap him.' Kurt's smile was self-congratulatory. 'As soon as I discovered that Wragg's people had been warned of my defection, I knew only one person could have passed on the information. Grisinger! And it was not difficult to discover that they *had* been warned.' In a scornful tone, he went on, 'They could not trouble to hide the fact of their knowledge. Their determination was only to find out why I had come. So I take them by the nose and make them think I am here because of this Ragnold. I even run to the court at the Old Bailey knowing they will follow like dogs at a hunt. I throw a piece of paper to let them think perhaps it is a secret message for their Ragnold which is just a lot of figures out of my head.' He gave a dry

157

chuckle. 'They think they bluff me and all the time I bluff them.'

'Very fine! It has gone well and soon you will be back in Berlin.'

'I go tomorrow night, you said?'

'Yes. The arrangements are now complete.'

'I fly?'

The big man shook his head. 'That is too dangerous. They are watching the airports. Even if we gave you different hair and a Mexican passport, it is still risky.' He grinned to reveal again a mouthful of gold capped teeth. 'No, my friend, you will be leaving England as a crate of machine tools, destination Poznan.' His grin widened at Kurt's expression. 'I explain. It is simple and it is safe. Close to Tower Bridge, there is moored the *Katowice II*. She is a Polish cargo ship sailing for Gdansk on the after-noon tide the day after tommorrow. Her cargo of machine tools will be loaded in the morning. It is only part of her cargo you understand. Most of it will be loaded tomorrow. The machine tools are coming from Birmingham in two lorries. These lorries will reach London tomorrow night and will be parked in a yard about a mile from the ship. During the night, one of the crates will be taken off and you inside a similar crate will be put on to the lorry in its place. As soon as you are on the ship, your crate will be opened and you will be free. All you have to do is stay out of sight until the ship is outside British waters.'

Kurt had listened with an expression of growing agita-tion. 'How big is this crate?'

'You will be able to sit in it with comfort. It has been specially made for you. It has a seat and, of course, holes for air and there will be a flask of water and some chocolate to eat if you are hungry. There is even a bottle for you to piss into.'

'How long shall I be inside?'

'Three hours perhaps. Not more. And,' the big man went on rather in the manner of a salesman, 'you cannot be turned upside down, because all the crates are carefully marked in English and Polish which way up they must be kept.'

'These air holes, won't they give it a different appearance from the others. Supposing someone notices?'

The big man shook his head reassuringly.

'They will not notice. You can hardly see the holes even when you know they are there. Everything has been thought of, my friend. Now, some more vodka?'

Kurt held out his glass, but still looked far from happy.

'I think it would have been simpler to fly.'

The big man frowned fleetingly. 'This is better. No one will suspect. No one will see you. You will go from here in a van and the transfer into the crate will take place behind locked gates.'

'Isn't there any guard on the lorries at night?'

'The man who owns the yard is one of our friends. I tell you that everything has been planned. Nothing will go wrong, if'—his tone carried a note of quiet warning—'you do as you are told. Your part is over; others have the responsibility of getting you out of the country. It is a time for trust—and obedience.'

Kurt shrugged. 'The sooner it is over, the better. But I do not like it.' He and the big man exchanged quick, suspicious glances.

Then the big man looked at his watch. 'I say goodnight to you, my friend. I shall be back tomorrow to supervise the smooth running of our arrangements.'

'What hour do we leave here?'

'At three o'clock in the morning. The lorry will drive out of the yard at six-thirty and you will be a free man on the ship in time to make a good breakfast.'

After he had gone, leaving behind a smell of cold mutton fat, Mikhail entered and made up the divan bed. For a while, Kurt sat and stared in deep thought at the wall opposite.

The prospect of being smuggled out as a crate of machine tools was no more pleasing to him now than it had been when first announced. It wasn't the discomfort which bothered him, nor even the risk of discovery which he now accepted as less than a more conventional mode of departure would be likely to incur. It was the indignity. But he realized that there was nothing he could do to alter the plans which had been made. He was a relatively small cog in the machine and, as the big man had pointed out, others had been given the responsibility of getting him safely out of England. His prior concurrence in the arrangements wasn't necessary—only, as he had also been brusquely reminded, his subsequent obedience.

It was funny to think that, just over twenty-four hours ago, he had been drinking Charles Ashmore's brandy. Now, though still technically in England, he had in effect left it for ever. He wondered whether Charles would bear him a lasting grudge for the deception he had practised on him. Being an Englishman with all those 'old school' virtues, he probably would. Not that the thought worried Kurt. What was much more important was that he had successfully accomplished what had been required of him. His lifelong friendship with Charles had proved useful in that, without it, the particular scheme could not have worked. But something else would then have been thought of. Perhaps, even, someone other than Kurt Menke would have had the central role. After all, it wasn't people who mattered, it was the system.

With this steadying thought, he got undressed and into bed. In the course of the night he dreamt he was already on the *Katowice II* and that the sea was rough. He woke up with a start to find that the divan had tilted and he was about to roll off.

The next day passed with painful slowness. Mikhail brought him some breakfast soon after eight o'clock and a little later came back with a couple of English newspapers. Kurt read these without finding any mention of himself. He hadn't expected to, as the only reason for Wragg's men to have courted publicity would have been if they wished to solicit public help in catching him. However, the fact that the newspapers were silent on what had happened didn't mean that nothing was being done to track him down. The way in which they had given the slip to Wragg's men in the car would have brought some heads close to the block and, more immediately, have caused a full-scale mobilization of effort to prevent him leaving the country.

After he had finished reading the papers, he went and

stood at the window and watched the rain coming down as though it were never going to stop. There must be grey cloud a hundred miles thick for as far as one could see, he reflected. The house had an unkempt garden and was surrounded by a high wall and the only sound was that made by the rain.

At noon, Mikhail brought him another tray of food and from then until the big man arrived soon after eight o'clock, Kurt spent the whole time lying on the divan staring at the ceiling.

The big man was in another of his cheerful moods.

'Soon now you will be home,' he said, after sending for the vodka and playfully cuffing Mikhail for forgetting the glasses. 'Glasses, quick! We're not peasants passing the bottle from mouth to mouth.'

'Anything further happened today?' Kurt enquired.

'No, not here. We have a report that someone went looking for Grisinger at his flat. A trap was laid for him, but he didn't return.'

'Who?'

'Gave the name of Pick and said he came from Leipzig.'

'A German?'

'He spoke fluent German, the report says. Enquiries are continuing.'

The evening dragged on and the rain which had let up but briefly had started again.

Kurt and the big man lapsed into silence as the minutes ticked by with the laboured effort of a dying man.

Kurt must have drifted off to sleep for he was suddenly aware that the big man was shaking him by the shoulder.

'It is time, my friend.'

'I must go to the lavatory.'

'All right, but don't take too long.'

The big man was waiting for him when he returned. He followed him down a passage to the back of the house and over into the yard, where a plain-sided blue van was parked.

'What happens if the police stop us?' he asked as the big man ushered him into the back and was about to close the doors.

'You can leave that to me,' the big man replied. He went

161

round to the front and got in beside the driver who was someone Kurt had not seen before.

It wasn't comfortable in the back of the van and Kurt was relieved when three quarters of an hour later they swung through a pair of high wooden gates which had been opened as they approached.

Apart from the discomfort, it had been an uneventful journey accomplished in complete silence apart from once when the big man, speaking in Russian, had obviously told the driver to moderate his speed.

As Kurt got out, he just had time to see the long, squat shapes of two laden lorries before he was hurried through a door into a wooden hut. There were three men already in the hut who stared at him with curiosity without, however, saying anything.

'The real crate of machine tools has already been taken off and we'll be taking that away in the van. Your crate is on the lorry and in a few minutes we'll go out and fasten you in.'

'I saw a cover over the crates,' Kurt said anxiously, 'I shall not be able to breath.'

The big man shook his head despairingly.

'You do not trust us to do anything correctly, do you, my friend? Your crate is the end one on the lorry, the tarpaulin covers the tops of the crates but it does not stretch over the end. Now, you are satisfied?'

Kurt nodded without any mark of enthusiasm.

'If you will take your jacket off for a minute——'

'Why?'

'The doctor here will give you a little injection. It is just to make you sleepy. It is like when you go on a journey and do not want to be sick. It will not harm you.'

The doctor nodded reassuringly and moved over to the table and opened his bag. Kurt eyed him suspiciously, but nevertheless took off his jacket and undid the button of his cuff.

'You are not going to drop dead,' the big man said heartily, 'it is just to make you feel more comfortable inside the crate. After the injection, we go outside and I show you everything.' He glanced at his watch. 'In half an hour we

162

must leave you. The driver will be here at six o'clock and you will arrive at the ship by seven. It is not far, but there are the various formalities to be undertaken. Customs and documentation.'

'Customs?' Kurt's voice had an anxious note. 'Supposing they examine the crate?'

The big man shook his head. 'They will only examine the documents. Perhaps they count the crates, but that is all.'

The doctor who had been standing by with a hypodermic syringe in hand indicated to Kurt that he should roll up his sleeve.

'See, you are still alive,' the big man said jovially when it was all over and Kurt had put his jacket back on. 'Now I show you everything.'

They went outside to the back of the nearer lorry. A small ladder had been placed there and Kurt followed the big man up. There was just room to stand between the two rear crates. The one on the right was open and Kurt peered into its dark interior.

'We cannot show a light,' the big man said. It is too dangerous. Give me your hand and I will show.' He grasped Kurt's wrist. 'This is where you sit,' he said, pushing Kurt's hand against what felt like a bicycle saddle. 'And here is a handle on each side to hold when the crate is loaded. Here is your water and here the chocolate. And here'—he plunged Kurt's hand down to the bottom of the crate behind the seat—'is for your toilet.'

'The air-holes? Where are the air-holes?'

'They are close to your head on each side. Here, feel. You will have plenty air and the holes are invisible from outside. Now, my friend, let me help you in and we will try it.'

With the big man giving a steadying hand, Kurt stepped into the crate and sat down on the saddle-type seat.

'It's O.K., yes?'

'Yes.'

The big man passed a hand across the top of the crate, level with where the lid would come.

'It is good. See. I do not touch your head.' He gave a

163

satisfied grunt. 'You are a perfect consignment of machine tools, my friend. It is fortunate that this load was waiting to go. It had to be a crate of the right size and our trade mission were able to help. We had two carpenters working all day to make it good for you.'

Kurt heard someone call out softly. The big man replied with a monosyllable, before turning his attention back to Kurt.

'The time has come. We place on the lid. But first I wish you good-bye and bon voyage.' He shook Kurt warmly by the hand. 'It will not be long that you must stay in here and then you will be free to enjoy your voyage home. All is O.K., yes?'

'Yes.'

The next moment the lid of the crate was placed in position and Kurt bit his lip in a sudden spurt of fear as he felt (rather than heard) it being screwed tight. He moved his head about gingerly and found that his hair brushed against the top of the crate. Putting out a hand, he felt for the air-holes, first on one side, then on the other. With equal caution he stretched his legs out into a more comfortable position.

When these exploratory manoeuvres were over, he found that his fear had somewhat abated. It was important that he should remain calm and do nothing to raise the temperature inside. The tarpaulin, which had been folded back, had obviously been replaced over the top of the crate and the darkness was as thick as molten tar. It seemed somehow increased by the absolute stillness that reigned. He had heard the van which brought him drive away and that had been the last sound to reach his ears.

He decided to have a drink of water. Anything was better than just sitting there contributing to the oppressive silence. His confidence went up a notch after he had found the flask, taken a drink from it and put it safely back in its holder.

To prevent his mind dwelling on all the things he could envisage going wrong, he began to count. He would count slowly up to a thousand. Long before he reached that figure, the lorry should be on its way. If it was not, something would have gone seriously wrong. But nothing would go wrong, he told himself. The big man and those for whom he worked were perfectionists at this sort of operation. Theirs was one of the most powerful organizations in the world. They didn't permit things to go wrong and they were especially diligent where their own kind were concerned. As the big man had said, nothing had been left to chance. Even now, the K.G.B.'s guardian angels were watching over him. He began to count——

He had reached three hundred and forty-seven when he thought he heard a sound outside. He paused and strained his ears. Yes, definitely someone was moving about the yard. Then there were voices. Comforting voices.

'I'd sooner sleep in the cab than that dump. You can 'ave a bird in the cab, too.'

'If you're lucky.'

'Luck ain't got nothing to do with it, mate. Anyway, you ready?'

Shortly after this, the lorry's engine rumbled into life and Kurt clutched at the handles either side of him as the driver revved up and the crate vibrated furiously.

For the first five minutes of the journey he held on for dear life, almost expecting to be thrown off at every depression in the road and at every corner they rounded. But then he became used to the rhythm of the lorry's movements and relaxed. It was like being on a choppy sea. Moreover, there couldn't really be any serious danger of his crate being cast off or the roads would be perpetually littered with cargo.

After about a quarter of an hour the lorry stopped, only to move forward a short distance and stop again. This time it was stationary for nearly half an hour. But at last the engine was restarted and they set off once more. The going was now extremely bumpy and Kurt reckoned that they must be in the dock area and be passing over cobbles and cables and sunken railway lines. He was obliged to hold on to the handles all the time to prevent himself being thrown from side to side.

The lorry came to a halt and he heard the unmistakable sound of a crane at work.

There were voices in his vicinity and he could tell from the sound that the tarpaulin was being lifted off. Some feeble light filtered its way through the air holes. Something landed on top of the crate with a crash and he ducked his head in alarm before realizing that it must be one of the lifting chains. There seemed to be hoarse shouts all about him and he scarcely dared breathe for fear he gave himself away. It seemed impossible that those who were separated from him by a mere layer of thin wood should be unaware of his presence.

He braced himself against the coming shock of lift off and was glad that he had done so as the crate gave a sudden crazy lurch to one side and then swung upwards like a feather caught in a draught. Up and up it went, swaying erratically while Kurt hung on. This was the worst part, but at least it was also the end of his ordeal.

Now the crate was being lowered, at first at an alarming speed, but now more slowly. He felt hands come out to steady it and then there was a bump as it touched down.

He sent up a small prayer of relief and relaxed. Soon he was aware of hands busying themselves with the lid. It was just as the big man had described.

There was a sound of wrenching wood and suddenly the grey light of early morning poured in.

Kurt looked up expectantly and found himself gazing at the impassive features of Wragg.

For several seconds they stared at one another, Kurt with a growing expression of uncomprehended defeat and Wragg with one of stony triumph. Then Kurt's eyes looked past Wragg at the wall of cargo behind which the crate had come to rest on the quayside. Over the top he could see the superstructure of a ship with men pointing in his direction and gesticulating. They might be friends and represent safety, but for all the good they were now able to do him they could just as well be the puppets they resembled. He raised his gaze to the cab of the crane which was responsible for his fate. One man was leaning impassively forward with folded arms, but a second man was half out of the window of the cab grinning happily as though he had just returned from the moon. Jerome Bowyer had been determined not to miss the act.

Kurt's eyes came back to Wragg who was still standing

patiently by. It was no more than a minute since the crate had been opened up, but, to Kurt, it seemed as though he had been through another life.

Wragg spoke. 'I'll give you a hand as I expect you're stiff.'

Thus captive and captor made their way to the waiting car looking, to those who now caught a first glimpse of them, like invalid and attentive nurse.

Kurt stared straight ahead of him and steadfastly refrained from glancing in the direction of the *Katowice II,* where the loading of her cargo of machine tools had just restarted.

CHAPTER XXVII

JEROME BOWYER telephoned Sarah at her office in the middle of the morning to tell her the news. He was obviously well pleased with himself and seemed in no way put out when she rejected his suggestion that they should meet for lunch.

'I felt almost sorry for Menke,' he said. 'Fancy thinking you're home and dry only to find yourself face to face with Wragg. Enough to put anyone off his breakfast.'

'What'll happen now?' Sarah asked.

'There'll be a long drawn-out period of feelers being cautiously extended via faceless intermediaries to see whether an exchange can be achieved. Menke for V.'

'And will it be achieved?'

'Depends on the relative values placed on the two items of merchandise in question. But I expect it'll come off, if only because both sides will be keen to show that they look after their own kind.'

Sarah was silent for a moment. Then she said in a faintly exasperated tone, 'When we were in Berlin, V's rescue meant everything to you. Now you speak of him as though he's an old newspaper.'

'That's not a bad simile,' Jerome said unabashed. 'He's certainly now no more use than an old newspaper. But you're wrong about my concern for his rescue. What I needed to find out was what had happened to him. Only then was it possible to draw the correct inferences. I never envisaged rescuing him.'

'Why do you make yourself sound so heartless?'

'I'm just realistic. Though I hope we can save V from a disagreeable fate.'

'But only in order to prove your omnipotence to all the others who run risks for you. Not on any humanitarian grounds.'

It was at this point that he had suggested their meeting for lunch and she had declined. Shortly afterwards he had rung off without reproach or sign of annoyance and had left Sarah to make strenuous, and largely unsuccessful, efforts to give her mind back to her work.

If necessary she told herself, she would move to Japan to avoid ever meeting him again. But even as this wild thought entered her head, her mind conjured up a picture of running into him on the Ginza or half-way up Mount Fuji, or wherever outrageous fate arranged these seemingly chance encounters on the other side of the world.

CHAPTER XXVIII

Two days later, Charles received a telephone call from Wragg.

'Would it be convenient to come and see you this afternoon?' he asked without any preliminaries.

'Half past three suit you?'

'Yes, I'll come then.'

Sarah had, of course, told her father of Kurt's detention, though she had been unable to satisfy his curiosity as to the background of the event or as to the whole mystery of Kurt's alleged defection.

Charles for his part had been feeling as high and dry as a piece of brushwood left behind by the receding tide. He had heard nothing since the evening when Kurt had dined at his house and made his disappearance.

But now Wragg was coming to see him and he determined that he shouldn't leave until he had learnt as much as he could properly expect to be told.

Promptly at half past three, Miss Acres announced that Wragg had arrived and a few seconds later showed him into Charles' office.

The two men shook hands gravely and Wragg sat down with the quick, tidy movements which characterized everything about him. It occurred to Charles who was watching him that he had the air of a client who had come to discuss his will rather than an officer of the British security service come to explain what a certain defection was all about. At least, that was what Charles hoped he had come to explain.

'We've found Menke,' Wragg said, fixing Charles with an intent stare, 'but perhaps you'd heard?'

'Where was he?' Charles asked, ignoring the invitation to disclose his own knowledge.

'He was about to be smuggled out of the country on a cargo ship.' In short, telegraphic sentences, Wragg proceeded to give Charles an account of Kurt's capture.

'It was pretty smart work getting on to him like that,' Charles observed.

Wragg shrugged. 'It was a question of assessing his most likely means of escape and then surveying the opportunities. It always struck me as likely that they'd try and smuggle him out as soon as they could make the necessary arrangements. Luckily for us there weren't many shipments that week which lent themselves to concealing a piece of human cargo. It became a matter of concentrating on the probabilities.'

'Another instance of routine enquiry, rather than dramatics, paying off.'

'Correct. Routine enquiry on a mammoth scale in this case. We mustered every man we could lay our hands on,

169

and I wasn't the only one who didn't get to bed for two nights. We had our men everywhere. The other side doesn't have a monopoly of infiltration, you know.'

'I'm sure it doesn't. But as a matter of interest, when did you first alight on Kurt's method of departure?'

'We had the two lorries under observation from the moment they left their factory in the Midlands.' With a faint grimace, he added, 'We also had a great number of other things and people under observation at the same time. It wasn't just a matter of luck——But I know you realize that.'

'Are you going to tell me what the whole thing was all about?'

Wragg's tone became more clipped. 'Menke was sent here to try and find out whether we had certain information.'

'We? Meaning the security service?'

'Correct.'

'And did he find out?'

'That's not for me to answer.'

'At all events, his was a bogus defection?'

'Correct.'

'And did Evelyn Ragnold figure in any of this?'

'No.'

'So you're now satisfied that his death was accidental?'

'He wasn't deliberately killed if that's what you mean.'

'It's rather more a question of what you mean.'

'I have no further comment.'

It was apparent to Charles that Wragg was sensitive to certain questions and he presumed this was because they tended to reflect on his own handling of the Menke affair. But, be that as it may, it seemed unlikely that he was going to learn a great deal more from this tight-lipped servant of the faceless guardians of the nation's security.

'Where is Kurt now?' he asked, beginning to wonder what was the reason for Wragg's visit.

'Staying in the country.'

'As your guest?'

'Correct.'

'Will he be brought before a Court?'

Wragg reacted as though he had received a sudden jab in the back. 'He hasn't been charged with any offence, so there's no need for him to appear in Court.'

Charles gave a faint shrug and looked away. 'Well, it's none of my business, anyway.'

He became aware of Wragg taking something out of his pocket.

'I have this letter for you.'

He held out an envelope and Charles took it. It was addressed to Mr. Charles Ashmore, 8 Edgeworth Terrace, London, S.W.3 and had an unfranked stamp in the top right-hand corner. Charles recognized Kurt's writing and turned the envelope over. It was sealed but not very securely. He gazed at it thoughtfully. A letter from Kurt which had obviously been intended for delivery by post, but which Wragg had brought by hand. It required no speculation to become certain that Wragg was aware of its contents.

Aware that his visitor was observing him keenly, he laid the letter down on his desk and then very deliberately pushed it to one side as though to indicate it could await attention later.

'You may wish to send back a reply,' Wragg remarked.

'You'd like me to open it?'

'It's up to you, but Menke would probably appreciate a reply and I can get it to him.'

Any lingering doubts Charles might have entertained as to whether Wragg had read the letter had been removed. At the same time, he found himself suddenly bored with the whole silly business. Wishing a plague on everyone's house, he picked up the envelope and slit it open. Inside was a single sheet of folded paper. He noticed that there was no address at the top, but that yesterday's date appeared. It read:

'My dear Charles,

I am being held here against my will. This is not legal. Please deal with my case and have me released. The courts and the newspapers must be told what is happening. Is not there in English law something called habeas corpus? Please invoke same for me. Must pray this letter arrives at you. Hasten please.

Kurt.'

He read the letter through a second time and then, with exaggerated care, he tore it into small pieces and dropped them into the waste-paper basket under Wragg's ever watchful gaze.

Looking up, he said:

'No, there isn't any reply.'

>>> If you've enjoyed this book and would like to discover more great vintage crime and thriller titles, as well as the most exciting crime and thriller authors writing today, visit: >>>

The Murder Room
Where Criminal Minds Meet

themurderroom.com

www.ingramcontent.com/pod-product-compliance
Ingram Content Group UK Ltd.
Pitfield, Milton Keynes, MK11 3LW, UK
UKHW040436280225
455666UK00003B/111